I0761818

What Rides at Night

Queer, Feminist, Fantastical Bicycle Halloween Stories

Edited by
Summer Jewel Keown

Elly Blue Publishing,
an imprint of Microcosm Publishing
Portland, OR + Cleveland, OH

What Rides At Night

Queer, Feminist, Fantastical Bicycle Halloween Stories

Edited by Summer Jewel Keown

First printing, September 9, 2025

ISBN 9781648414527
This is Microcosm # 879
Cover art by Gerta Egy
Design by Joe Biel and Sarah Koch

This is Bikes in Space Volume 13
For more volumes visit BikesInSpace.com
For a catalog, write or visit:

Microcosm Publishing
2752 N Williams Ave.
Portland, OR 97227

All the news that's fit to print at www.Microcosm.Pub/Newsletter
Get more copies of this book at www.Microcosm.Pub/WhatRidesatNight

EU Safety Information: https://microcosmpublishing.com/gpsr

Global labor conditions are bad, and our roots in industrial Cleveland in the '70s and '80s made us appreciate the need to treat workers right. Therefore, our books are MADE IN THE USA.

Microcosm's workers and authors are paid solely from book sales. If you downloaded this book from some sketchy part of the Internet or picked up what appears to be a bootleg, please support our hardworking team by purchasing a copy directly from us and encouraging your communities to do the same. Paying for our books and zines helps us publish work that's far better than anything AI can come up with. Additionally, an MIT study revealed that AI inhibits humanity's critical thinking ability. Since critical thinking is one of our core values, we prohibit any use of our books to "train" generative artificial "intelligence" (AI) technologies, because seriously, WTF.

Library of Congress Cataloging-in-Publication Data

Names: Keown, Summer Jewel, 1981- editor | Blue, Elly editor
Title: What rides at night : queer, feminist, fantastical bicycle halloween stories / by Summer Jewel Keown (editor) & Elly Blue (series editor).
Description: Portland, OR : Microcosm Publishing, 2025. | Series: Bikes in space ; 13 | Summary: "Gather 'round, ghoulfriends, and peer into this enchanting collection of ghost stories, tall tales, and feminist fictions simmering with cyclist power. When the veil thins, the bicycle revolution rises. Thirteen new, original, spooky stories for the thirteenth volume the Bikes in Space series!"-- Provided by publisher.
Identifiers: LCCN 2025028954 | ISBN 9781648414527 trade paperback
Subjects: LCSH: Science fiction, American | Ghost stories, American | Feminist fiction, American | Cycling--Fiction | Halloween--Fiction | LCGFT: Short stories
Classification: LCC PS648.S3 W395 2025
LC record available at https://lccn.loc.gov/2025028954

About the Publisher

Elly Blue Publishing was founded in 2010 to focus on feminist fiction and nonfiction about bicycling. In 2015, Elly Blue Publishing merged to become an imprint of Microcosm Publishing that is still fully managed by Elly Blue.

Microcosm Publishing is Portland's most diversified publishing house and distributor, with a focus on the colorful, authentic, and empowering. Our books and zines have put your power in your hands since 1996, equipping readers to make positive changes in their lives and in the world around them. Microcosm emphasizes skill-building, showing hidden histories, and fostering creativity through challenging conventional publishing wisdom with books and bookettes about DIY skills, food, bicycling, gender, self-care, and social justice. What was once a distro and record label started by Joe Biel in a drafty bedroom was determined to be *Publishers Weekly*'s fastest-growing publisher of 2022 and #3 in 2023, and is now among the oldest independent publishing houses in Portland, OR, and Cleveland, OH. We are a politically moderate, centrist publisher in a world that has inched to the right for the past 80 years.

CONTENTS

INTRODUCTION

Queerly beloved, ride up and gather around tonight's crackling bonfire for a tale of Halloween. Thirteen tales, to be exact.

I've always loved Halloween (or All Hallows' Eve, or Samhain) because anything can happen when the veils between the worlds are thin. Ghost stories feel like those ghosties could be waiting for us just there, in the shadows, and we shiver with fearful delight. Witches' spells might really enspell and entrance us. The spirits may tell us truths through any manner of divination. We run through the halls of haunted houses and corn mazes that threaten to get us lost forever. It's all for the thrill, and we're perfectly safe, we think, but maybe, just maybe . . .

As a kid, the highlight of my Halloween was climbing into the straw-filled tractor of the haunted hayride that would take us out into the pitch-black night, where the Headless Horseman would inevitably ride by. I'd hold tight to the edge with one hand and peek through the other hand's fingers, delightfully terrified of this shadowy figure atop a dark horse racing just alongside us, his eyes glowing orange in the night, sure that he was looking right at me. We survived with our heads, just barely, to do it all again the next year. But there was always the possibility that one Halloween, he would finally catch up.

Halloween is, and has always been, for the queers, the weirdos, the rebels, those of us who haven't and don't want to fit neatly into any of the boxes that sit waiting to trap us inside. It's the one holiday where we can be anyone we've always imagined, as long as we can figure out a costume for it. We can try it on for a night and revel in this version of us, while wearing the cloak of plausible deniability until we're ready to be ourselves all the time. On Halloween, we can trick, treat, and be spooky with ghosts, witches, monsters, and other role models.

In this time where reading the news each day can be a series of jump scares, we have to ride together to keep our beautifully wild and queer community safe, to bring each other joy, and to be the perfectly wonderful monsters we want to see in the world.

I was first a reader of the ***Bikes in Space*** series, then a writer, and now, thanks to Elly Blue for entrusting me with this volume, a guest editor. I fell in love with each story as they were shared with us by their authors. The characters are trans, ace, gay, bi, pan, any and all flavors of the queer rainbow, but what they all have in common is riding into that Halloween Eve on two wheels and finding something for themselves there. I hope you'll find something for yourself too.

Summer Jewel Keown
Saint Paul, Minnesota
Halloween 2025

ENTROPY

NELL HANSON

5

Nobody walked my path through the woods. I'd never seen anyone on it, at least; it was always just me and the trees and the undergrowth so thick you couldn't get through it without tearing yourself to pieces. These woods weren't made for human consumption, I'd learned.

I found the bike on my third straight day of walking my path. The longest I'd gone before turning back was a week, at which point everything turned black, so I'd definitely passed by here before. I'd never seen anything man-made in the woods, and this bicycle with its sunshine-yellow paint would never have escaped my attention before, which meant only one thing: someone had been here in the last couple days.

"Hello?"

My voice echoed despite the thick smothering of the wood. When nobody answered, I sagged a little with relief, then pushed through the sharp tangle of dry branches to inspect the thing closer.

It might have been pretty once. It was one of those retro-looking bikes with brown trim and a basket, but it lay on its side with a bent wheel, two flat tires, and rust on every inch of exposed metal—which was quite a bit, considering the state of the peeling yellow paint. Moss grew through cracks in the seat. It must have been there for ages. No one rode this thing into the woods in the last week.

I couldn't shake the feeling that I should have seen it before. I knew this path like it was my life; I knew it better than I knew myself.

I sat down in the leaves and stared at the bike. If it was on my path, it belonged to me now. No one would be able to get it out of here, anyway, even if it had two good wheels.

I put my hand down to brace myself to stand, but it landed on something hard and smooth rather than the cushion of loam I expected. I thought it must have been a large stone, but when I lifted it to get a better look, it looked back.

The skull was in good condition—cleaned by birds and insects, but sheltered enough by the thick wood to remain intact except for a large dent above the left eye, which I guessed must have been what killed the poor girl. I brushed my thumb over the cheekbone and hummed. This was mine, now, too.

She was beautiful.

4

I kept walking after my discovery, but I found myself returning to it a few days later. I'd left the skeleton where I'd found it—what else could I do?—but I wanted to see it again.

Something looked different as I approached the bicycle. It looked . . . better. Not *good*, and certainly not clean, but I was fairly certain the entirety of the fork had been rusted the last time I saw it. Now, it was half covered in that pretty yellow paint, dirty as it was.

Maybe I was mistaken, and at first I thought I must have been, but I rummaged in the leaves for the skull and shrank back when I touched something wet and moving.

Maggots? But the bone had already been picked clean. I plucked one into my hand to be sure, and sure enough, the small white creature wriggled on my palm as if it wanted to feed on me, too. I returned it to its meal and kept walking.

3

I couldn't stay away for long. I did try to forget about the abandoned things in the woods. But that skull called my name when I was away, and her voice was so sweet and lonely. How could I leave her out there by herself? I didn't like being out there alone, either.

I had to guess it was about a couple days before I found my way back. The first thing I should have noticed was the shiny paint on the bike, only slightly rusted now on the handlebars and the spokes of the wheels. But what I saw first was the crown of the skull poking above the layer of dead leaves, wearing a wreath of maggots and hair.

Yes, she had some remnants of hair now. It was dirty, but I thought it was probably a strawberry-blond color underneath the grime. The maggots were busy working out from the wound on her forehead and had ignored much of the rest of her. Her skeleton was intact this time, held together by what was left of her flesh. Her face was too blackened and taut to be recognizable, but I still thought she was beautiful. It was too bad her eyes were gone, but maybe I'd get to see them later. I couldn't say why, but I imagined they would be a pretty blue-gray.

2

I slept next to my friend for the next few days and watched as she slowly, steadily got better. Her shriveled, decayed limbs started plumping back up. Her swollen abdomen gradually fell back to where it belonged. Her face looked more like a face, and I could almost recognize it if only I could remember.

Her dress was nice. Once the tatters sewed themselves back together enough, I could tell it was a yellow sundress that matched the bike, which by now looked almost new save for the one bent wheel. She must have loved that bike to bring it out here and die with it.

1

I couldn't keep track of how long it took before she looked nearly whole. Nearly alive. If I blurred my eyes a bit, she could have been sleeping despite the blood smeared across her face. It could have been my lipstick.

I could almost taste her name in my mouth. It started with a K, I was certain, but I couldn't summon more than that. All I knew was that my chest ached looking at her, and I wanted to weave her hair into twin braids; I wanted to kiss her strawberry lips; I wanted her to hold me in her lap after a picnic on a nice spring afternoon. It was spring now, judging by the vibrant green around us. We must have skipped winter somehow.

The picnic lay scattered around the bike basket: a moldy loaf of bread, containers of deli meat, a few apples with dimples and bruises in their skin but almost looking edible. They'd been mush a week or so ago.

Funny. My path was never a visible one, but now I could see bare earth where I'd walked for so long. A thin strip, just wide enough for one person, or for the tread of a bicycle.

0

My bike returned toward the end. It was red, and I remembered now: it was a gift from my parents. I'd last seen it seven days into the woods, but now it was back and on its side next to its yellow friend. Kate's fresh blood oozed up her dress, up her neck, up her face; up, up into her wound.

She even breathed now. She'd been alive for a little while after the crash, and I only hoped she didn't feel the pain. No one knew these woods; no one used them but us. She was never going to make it out, no matter how hard I tried to get help. And I tried. But it's easy to get lost in these woods in a panic, and it's not like anyone knew where to look for us.

Everything would be all right, though. Kate was almost healed, and we'd get back on our bikes, and we would go back to the start. All we'd have ahead of us now was a bright spring day, wind tangling our hair, a picnic on the horizon.

The Ghosts Ride with Us

Erin Cullen

Val broke up with me because the first time she invited me to join a New Moon Ride, I laughed in her face. "I am *not* a Rider," I said, once I finished laughing. That seemed like all the explanation that could possibly be required.

"None of us are born Riders," Val replied. "I just started showing up a year ago. It's a great group. Mostly women, mostly queer, but they welcome everyone."

"Everyone brave enough to ride a bicycle through a cemetery full of angry ghosts, you mean."

"It isn't as bad as it sounds. When you're with the Ride, it's a completely different experience."

"No way. I'm not a Rider. If you pass by me, I'll cheer you on."

Val looked at me with a disappointment that had become familiar already in our brief relationship. I had liked her imagination, at the beginning. She seemed to want to spend her life having the adventures of a character in a comic book, and the way she talked about things like the monthly Ride had enchanted me on our early dates. But then she started inviting me to do those crazy things with her. I told her no again and again. Apparently the Ride was the last straw, because two days after that conversation she texted me to say that she'd been thinking it might be best if we stopped seeing each other. *You live in a very limited world*, she said. *If that's what you want, this isn't going to work out.*

I was offended that she'd called not wanting to risk my life on the Ride *living in a very limited world* and hurt by the abruptness of the text, so I told her that no longer seeing each other was perfectly fine with me. I only realized after we'd gone our separate ways that maybe she wasn't only talking about the Ride.

Without Val, my life was boring. My days were all the same. That had never been a problem before, but when I was with Val, I'd lived life at least at the fringes of adventure. I had felt like I was always trying to catch up to her, but most of the time, I'd been eager to do it. Maybe, a part of me had thought, I was capable of catching up to her once and for all. The quiet and stillness of my life without her had become unbearable.

So here I am: at the door of the warehouse where the Riders meet, twenty minutes before sunset on the night of a new moon.

I hear voices inside the warehouse and recognize Val's. She had sent out a message earlier in the week saying that the Riders were recruiting, but I doubt she expects to see me after the way we ended things. I wondered at first if she had included me in the message by mistake, but I'd decided that it didn't matter. I had come, in the end, because I miss Val. I miss the excitement of being around her. I miss the look she gets on her face whenever I do something surprising, and riding into that warehouse is a surefire way to elicit it.

That's what I'm thinking about as I coast on my bike through the warehouse's gaping door. The interior is big enough for a crowd of hundreds, but much of the floor space is taken up by rows of bikes, stands for bike repair, and shoulder-high chests of tools. The voices come from an open space in the center stocked with well-used couches, tables, and a mini-fridge, an oddly comfortable human space in a building designed for the metal and mechanical.

Val leaps up from one of the couches as I ride in. "Jamie!" She sounds thrilled, and the earnest excitement in her voice sends a pang of warmth through me. Val's face is streaked with glitter, cerulean and gold strips of it spanning up and out across her cheeks like a bird's wings. I've never seen her done up like this before, but somehow she looks exactly like herself. Her eyes are bright and excited under shimmering gold shadow, lined boldly to compete with the sparkles bouncing light from her cheeks. As always, I feel boring and plain next to her, but I force a smile as I dismount near the couches and engage the kickstand on my bike. It's easy to see that this is a safe place to leave it out in the open and unlocked.

"I'm so glad you're here," Val says, smiling big enough to scrunch the streaks of glitter on her face. She steps forward and hugs me. I guess we hug each other now. The helmet I haven't had a chance to take off bumps awkwardly into her shoulder before I step back.

"Thanks for inviting me," I say, as if there's no more to it. Now that Val has seen me, the reality of being here starts to settle in. I'm actually going to Ride. Val has a fistful of stories about close calls—the music that sustains the Ride cutting out due to a battery failure and being replaced with breathless a capella singing, a Rider who had fallen out of the Ride's ring of magic and had to be carried on the back of someone else's bike while inconsolable after getting swarmed, a cemetery so thick with the ghosts' shadowy presence that the Riders couldn't even see the edges of the road. I look around at the dismal crowd—three people sit chatting with each other on the couches and two more stand near one of the tables. The table looks like it was set up for a kindergarten art class, even though the Ride hasn't let kids join for decades. Mostly women, mostly queer, like Val once told me. "I guess I'm a little early."

Val's smile freezes in place, then disappears. "You're right on time," she says. "Come on, let's get you some glitter."

"I'm not really a face-painting type," I say, not following Val toward the table.

"Preach," a woman on the couch says. She's old enough to be my mother, with gray hair shorn short. Her face is bare of paint and makeup both, her unadorned features nevertheless sharp and confident. I wish I could look like that—I can't stand to leave home without at least foundation, eyeliner, and mascara.

Val turns back to me. "Just a little? It's part of the magic."

"If she doesn't want to wear it, she doesn't have to," the same gray-haired woman says.

"Alicia, you don't wear it because you don't like the way it feels, and that's fine, but Jamie doesn't want to wear it because it looks weird," Val says. She turns to me and raises her eyebrows, an expectant expression familiar from the debates we use to have about makeup and the like. "Right?"

I roll my eyes—I've been here maybe two minutes, and Val is already poking at one of the few topics we never could agree on. Val uses makeup for fun—for sport, almost—but for me, wearing makeup is about dignity. I don't want anyone to think less of me for my plain features when the tools to modify them are readily available. Val doesn't understand that some people have to care about the way we look. We don't have whatever Val has inside her that lets her move through the world like her body is hers alone, rather than an object that exists for other people, too.

"You don't have to," Val says. I want to be glad for her easy concession, but I'm too focused on the disappointment in her voice.

"Is it really part of the magic?" If it's important, I suppose I can stomach it. I'm supposed to be trying to be a Rider, after all.

I hear a 'Yes' and a 'No' at the same time, from Val and Alicia respectively.

"It's complicated," says one of the women at the table. She's older than me but younger than Alicia, with cornrowed hair that reaches past her waist. She turns to me. "Hi. I'm Imani. I ride in front with the boombox."

"I know," I say, then I cringe. Maybe it's weird to admit that I recognize her from New Moon Rides that have passed by my window over the years. "I'm Jamie."

"I heard," Imani says, sending Val a quick smile before turning her gaze to a mirror on the table and going back to dabbing sparkling crimson dots on a silver field smattered on one of her cheeks. "Anyway, the answer as to whether the glitter is magic is *it depends*. If it makes you feel good, it's part of the magic. There's not much difference between magic and feeling out there. You'll see."

The *you'll see* freezes up my insides. I'm really here, about to join the Riders on a New Moon Ride. The *six* Riders—no one else has come in behind me. I had been expecting a crowd of dozens, a crowd I could get lost in. But instead, it seems like it really matters whether or not I put on the stupid glitter. It matters how I feel, because my feelings are going to be an unignorable portion of the Ride's magic. And what I feel is stiff and scared, and like I really, *really* don't belong here.

I don't know what I'd expected when I heard from Val that the Riders were recruiting, but it certainly wasn't this level of desperation. "I actually don't know if I'm going to go after all," I say. It's still a little before sunset. I could leave in the next few minutes and be safe in my apartment before the slips reach town and swarm anyone left on the street. "I don't usually bike at night, and I've been having issues with my brakes."

I had been trying to make excuses to leave, but Alicia leaps up from the couch. "Let me take a look."

"I'm taking it to a mechanic later this week," I lie.

"It'll just take a sec." Alicia grabs a box of tools from a cluttered workbench and gestures me toward one of the bike stands surrounding the couches.

It would be rude to turn her down at this point, so I wheel my bike over and let her hoist it up onto the stand. "Thanks."

"The Ride isn't as scary as it looks from the outside," she says as she manually spins the front wheel and squeezes the brakes. "Your brake pads are too far out. I'll tighten them and you can go for a quick test ride around the track before we get going. Anyway, we probably won't even make it into the cemetery tonight."

"What?" Val sounds as appalled as she'd been when I told her I hadn't had my bike tuned up in four years. She's standing near the glitter table now, as if she can draw me over with the force of her presence. "We've never skipped the cemetery two months in a row."

"Look around, kid. We've got seven Riders including a rookie, and we *did* skip it last month, which means it's going to be packed to the corners with ghosts. We won't make it through."

"Then what happens next month?" Val asks. "And don't you dare say the town lights weaken slips enough that the new moon isn't a problem anymore."

"I would *not* say that," Alicia says, her voice sharp as if reprimanding Val for implying that she could possibly support the plan to light the town well enough to solve the ghost problem for good. The most populated areas have been installing street lights big and bright enough to make night and day almost indistinguishable. "But we can't control what happens next month. We're Riders, and we can't Ride if we do something dangerous and get hurt."

"It's really sounding like it's not a good night for me to join," I say, even as Alicia lifts my bike down from the stand and pushes it back toward me. "I'll just slow you down."

"We ride at a pace that works for everyone," Imani says. "We don't worry about speed."

"I didn't mean just biking."

"Take that test ride," Alicia says. She gestures me toward the outer wall of the warehouse, where a track is marked with lines of duct tape on the floor. "You need a better front light."

"I have spares," the one guy in the room says. He reaches into a hefty backpack resting on the floor next to him and emerges with a light still in its packaging, which he holds out to me.

"Thanks, Mike," Imani says.

"I can't—" *I can't do this*. I can't imagine any flashlight that would make a meaningful dent in the darkness I'm about to ride into. "The one I have is fine. And we'll be biking in a group, so it doesn't matter, right?"

"It matters," Imani says shortly.

"Please ride your bike around in a circle," Alicia says.

I accept the light from Mike and drop it in the basket on the back of my bike rather than admit to these people that I don't know how to install it.

Wanting to please Alicia, I get on and start to pedal around the track, testing the brakes whenever I get up enough speed. I can now jerk the bike to a stop instead of slowly losing speed when I clench the brake against the handlebar, but it's hard to control my speed with my sweaty, shaking hands. Still, it's reassuring to know that I won't accidentally slide into traffic if I'm riding too fast—though of course we're not going to encounter any traffic on a New Moon Ride.

While pedaling around the track, I catch a glimpse of the sky from the warehouse's open door. The last rays of red from the sunset are disappearing, the sky night-gray beyond the artificial glow from the town's new streetlights. I jerk the bike to a stop, blinking as if that can make the colors come back. But no. It's too late for me to leave. I'd been counting on the Ride clearing away enough of the slips to be safe biking home later, but now I'm not sure I'll be able to get home safely at all.

I coast back over to the couches. I'd rather be overrun by ghosts than ask if it's okay for me to just stay here for the night. "It works great. Thanks," I say to Alicia.

Alicia nods in satisfaction.

"We'll head out in five," Imani says.

My hands are clammy and my heart thuds urgently against my ribcage. Desperate for distraction, I look at Val, who's still leaning against the table. She catches my eye and straightens, hopeful.

I take a tentative step toward her, then another. If I'm going to be biking with the Riders, I may as well look like one.

"Color?" Val asks, eager.

"You pick," I say. I see her grin, her glitter sparkling against the warehouse's artificial lights, then I shut my eyes.

I feel better about the whole thing as soon as Val touches me. The pads of her fingers are warm and soft on my cheeks as she paints them with a layer of sticky gel. She's never done my makeup before, but it's certainly not the first time she's touched my face, and the familiarity of her deft touch warms something inside me and quiets the fear.

I wonder now if she thought of me personally, or if the Riders were so desperate she sent the message to everyone on her contact list who owns a bicycle.

But I showed up, and to these people, not even just Val, that seems to matter.

Val paints a design that feels like the one on her own face, long streaks of glitter going up and out like wings. I hope it's magic, like Val says. I'm going to need all the help I can get.

"Jamie, what kind of music do you like?" Imani asks while my eyes are still closed.

"Pop, mostly. The classics."

"Throw some old-school One Direction on there," Val says.

I jolt. The New Moon Riders did *not* need to know that I still have a soft spot for my favorite boy band from middle school.

"Hold still," Val admonishes. She's dotting glitter onto the streaks of gel now.

Imani chuckles. "Any other requests for the playlist?"

A few people call out song titles, mostly the classics I'd been assuming we'd Ride to. The titles I don't know are probably from bands much cooler than One Direction.

"I'm finished," Val says. When I open my eyes, Val is still standing very close to me, close enough that her hip brushes against mine as she reaches across the table for a makeup mirror. "Look."

"No," I say quickly, "I don't want to see it." If I don't look, I don't have to know what other people see when they look at me. At least if anyone I know sees me on the Ride, they aren't likely to recognize my face.

Val retracts her hands. "Well, you look amazing." Her expression flickers, a rare slip in her confidence. "Not that you didn't already! I'm not just . . . complimenting my own glitter skills."

"I'm sure it's great," I say, bumping my hip against hers on purpose this time. I know Val is as human as anyone, but it feels odd to reassure her, and odder still to see her relax in response. I'm not used to seeing her caring about anyone's opinion of her, but I guess she cares about mine.

Val smiles, then turns back to the table, tossing all the art supplies into a box. "Do you need anything? Water?"

"I brought water."

"Great." She smiles, and looks at me for long enough that it feels like it means something. "I'm really glad you're here."

I laugh, not sure what else to do with the burst of warmth that pokes into the knotted ball of worry in my chest. "That makes one of us."

"Everyone is," Val says. "Not just the other Riders, the rest of town, too. No one's wanted to join up recently because it seems like the lights are working, but they're not going to keep the ghosts out of town forever. Nothing ever does, except the Ride."

"I know that." Everyone does. The lights are a stopgap, like the men who used to march out to the edge of town on new moons to fend off the ghosts with torches and fireworks, leaving the women at home to protect the children and elderly. But even in the earliest days, there had been slips, ghosts powerful enough to break through the first line of defense and haunt the town until sunrise. Fires in hearths had been enough to keep the slips out of homes, and then it hadn't. So, the women had started building bonfires in the streets, and the gatherings around the fires had become like parties; the women soon realized that joyful celebration repelled the ghosts far more effectively than huddling around a fire in terror. But eventually, even the bonfires weren't enough. Groups, lit with lanterns and held together by song, started gathering for marches. All the while, the men kept trying to beat ghosts back at the border of the town, a tactic that hadn't worked in years.

Marches turned into the Ride as soon as bicycles became popular, which was well before it was acceptable for a woman to ride one. The early Riders defied their fathers and husbands to join a Ride that blazed light and music through the town, sweeping the ghosts up with it and leaving the streets peaceful for the rest of the night. The first Ride was over a hundred years ago. The town has no one left alive to remember it, but it's stayed mostly a women's endeavor—and lately a queer one—because somehow, men are still mad about it.

It's a legacy so large I can't imagine taking it on. But here I am.

Val grins. I don't know if she even realized I meant that I am not glad I'm here. I don't want to go out in the dark and the cold and try to be part of a magic I don't understand. But the sky outside beyond the central lights is already dark, and Imani is walking a bike I recognize toward the entrance. The frame is wrapped with strands of tiny lights, and pieces of tinsel are twisted into the spokes of the wheels, tightly enough that there's no danger of them coming loose. A two-wheeled cart attached to the back of the bike holds the boombox, which looks even bigger and heavier up close. I don't know how Imani stays upright dragging it along, and I'm suddenly glad that I'm not the one who has to deal with it. At that moment, it feels like the least I can do is follow her to the entrance.

Val brings her bike up next to mine. I avoid her eyes as I strap my helmet back on and mount the seat. I don't want her to see how scared I am. I focus on Imani, sitting tall and proud on her bike as she looks out at the paltry few rest of us. "Ready?" she asks.

"Ready," some of the others say.

She presses a button on the boombox. The opening chords of "Don't Stop Believin'" blast through the speaker, echoing from the high metal walls of the warehouse, making me want to start dancing in spite of my fear of what awaits us outside. The Rider in front of me turns on their lights. I copy them, only then remembering that

I never figured out how to install the new light Mike had so kindly given me. Stupid and rude.

"I said, *are you ready*?" Imani shouts over the music. All thoughts of my rudeness leave my head. There's only the music, my bike, my muscles that will power it, the cluster of other bikes and Riders around me, Val grinning at my side.

"Ready!" I shout, along with every single one of the others. The sound echoes from the walls. Imani nods in satisfaction, then leads us out of the warehouse, our music and light spilling onto the street outside.

We've ridden less than a block when I start to hear the cheers. We're starting in the heart of town, riding through the odd fake daylight streaming from the huge lamps towering over every street corner. Blackout curtains, installed on just about every window in town to block the floodlights, are flung open just for us. The people here have nothing to fear on new moons these days, but they're still cheering for the Riders bringing music and magic through their neighborhoods. And I'm in the middle of the pack, looking like one of them.

Like Imani had assured me, I have no trouble keeping up with the pace. The music seems to vibrate through the frame of my bike into my skin, my strokes of the pedals automatically adjusting to the beat along with those of everyone around me. I'm at the center of the pack, next to Val, not touching any of the Riders around me but nonetheless linked together as if we're a single organism. Even the cheers that occasionally meet us from the buildings feed the feeling of rightness that holds all of us together.

We stay in the well-lit neighborhoods around the warehouse for a surprisingly long time, so long it feels silly to have our bike lights shining ineffectively out into the brightness around us. I feel powerful, unstoppable. I forget that I was ever afraid.

Then Imani leads us past an unlit street corner, out into growing darkness. It's easy enough to keep my focus on the Ride for the first block. Our pack is a flaming mass of music and light and life I'm snug in the middle of, letting me ignore the darkness around us.

Then something brushes past me, slicing through the Ride with dark and cold and silence. It lasts a fraction of a moment, quickly repelled by the barrier of magic we've built around ourselves. The intrusion of the first slip is what it takes for me to realize that the barrier exists, fragile and intangible and wholly dependent on seven people on bikes, including me with no idea what I'm doing. This is the *Ride*, the town's first defense against the ghosts that flood in from the cemetery every new moon to drag humanity down into the dark with all the power they can get their hands on. If our magic isn't stronger than theirs, we're stuck out here, easy targets, horrifically vulnerable.

The air is thick with ghosts now. Another slip cuts through the light, and then a swarm of them pushes in for a heartstopping few seconds of darkness and silence.

I want to go home. But if I leave the Ride now, I'll never make it.

Something cool and soft touches my arm. I startle before I realize that it's just Val's hand, chilled from riding into the wind. "You've got this," she shouts. The anxiety in her eyes betrays the encouragement of her words.

I cringe away from her. I know why she said it. I am slowing them down. Not physically, but magically. I'm not a Rider. I don't belong here.

There's a long silence from the boombox. Maybe my presence is going to ruin everything. I should never have come.

Then I hear just a moment of music, familiar enough for me to recognize it in a single beat. Old-school One Direction. On the playlist only because Val knew I would enjoy it, and Imani wanted something on the playlist for me.

Maybe I can't believe that I ought to be here, but the others believe I do. Not just Val and Imani, but Alicia and Mike who were so kind to me, and the way all of them have wrapped me in the middle of their cluster, making certain I won't be left behind. They've treated me like one of the Riders, and all they expect of me in return is to act like one.

No one else here can feel the magic of "Best Song Ever" like I can. I stand up on my pedals so I can do something closer to dancing, and start to sing along with the lyrics. My voice wobbles and I almost choke on the words, and then Val stands up too, just in time to lean toward me with a cheeky "*Ow!*" Imani grins and reaches down to turn the volume on the boombox a touch higher.

I can feel the beat pulsing through my veins. It's way too loud for me to be self-conscious about my off-key voice as Val and I sing and dance on our pedals. The magic surges, flowing around us in shining, sparkling warmth. We're so much more than a streetlight. We're a sun.

The song ends, but the magic holds steady. I let myself take some credit for it. I played my role. My love of the music of my childhood had sustained us for a few minutes, and I understand now what Imani meant when she said that feeling and magic are pretty much the same thing out here. I let myself feel the joy and peace and community of being one of the Riders, and I see it flowing out into the bubble of magic around us, letting us ride right through the wispy forms of ghosts in our path.

Imani holds out a hand, signaling for us to slow down. I'm confused until I see that there's a light ahead of us on the road. It's certainly not the only light we've seen since leaving the bright center of town behind—some people have installed streetlights in their own yards, hoping that they can at least keep ghosts away from their homes—but it's the only light we've seen *moving*. I hadn't thought there was anyone around here stupid enough to try to drive a car after sunset on a new moon.

The motion of the light makes it obvious why. The headlights of the car aren't approaching steadily, they're jiggling from side to side, as if the human at the steering wheel is fighting against malevolent ghosts for control. If we're not careful, the car could hit us. Our magic isn't built to repel a two-ton hunk of metal moving toward us at speed. But we're the Ride—we can't leave the humans in that car to fend for themselves.

The headlights approach, and my fear resurges. I try to transform it into protectiveness, bolstering the magic, and strength, pumping my legs on the pedals. I can't tell if it works. The Ride rearranges itself into a single file line. I'm in front of Val, behind Alicia. I'm afraid and engaged, determined. I'm one of the Riders. I hold my spot.

The car is still moving unsteadily, zigzagging across the road. Ahead of Alicia, Imani increases her speed. The rest of us follow. We approach the car, and the car approaches us. It passes close enough for me to touch, and I barely resist looking behind me to make sure it hasn't hit Val. Seconds later, we're past it, and Imani is slowing down, circling back to the car, turning down the volume on the boombox enough that we'll be able to hear each other speak. The bubble of magic around us trembles a little but holds steady.

The car stopped just ahead of where we passed by it. Two people stumble out of the front seat. Ironically, there are two hardy mountain bikes strapped to the car's roof.

"Are you both alright?" Imani asks when she reaches them.

One of them, a man, nods, then looks at his companion. She nods too, a little shakily.

"What the hell were you thinking, driving out here tonight?" Imani asks.

"We misjudged the time," the woman says, reaching out to cling to her companion's hand. "We thought we'd be back before sunset."

"It's hard to remember when sunset is anymore," the man explains. "We live in town."

"I hate to ask, but will you escort us home?" the woman asks.

Next to me, Val grimaces. I can tell that escorting a car back into town would be a drain on the magic of the Ride, and we still haven't gone anywhere near the cemetery.

"Or you could come with us," I say. "Pick up the car tomorrow. We're not too far out from town."

The woman laughs, startled. "We're not Riders."

"I wasn't either, before tonight."

The man looks around, clearly thinking about it. He frowns. "We don't have lights."

"I have an extra," I say.

"So do I," says Mike, reaching around to retrieve one from his apparently bottomless backpack of supplies.

The strangers look at each other, coming to a joint decision in silence in the way only people who know each other well can. "Alright," the woman says, turning to the rest of us. "Let's do this."

They get their bikes down from the roof rack and retrieve helmets from the car. Mike and Alicia help them install the spare lights. We're starting back down the road before the next song starts, a more robust group of nine.

I can tell that we're aiming for the general direction of the cemetery now. The black of night and the ghosts that hide within it hover close to our bubble, but the magic is too strong now to flicker at their presence. There are cheers from apartment complexes we pass by. This time, I feel the encouragement they're trying to provide. I'm one of the Riders. The cheers are meant for me, too. They go through me and out into the magic around us via my steady breaths, the pulse of my legs on the pedals, the glances I exchange with the other Riders to check in and stay in sync. I smile at Val, and she grins back at me. I imagine that I look brave and powerful, with whatever glitter design she painted on my face. I feel stronger than I ever have in my life.

There's a tangible change when we pass through the gates into the cemetery. I know that the stars don't actually wink out, that the darkness above us is nothing more than a thick layer of ghosts clustered here, the same ghosts we've been driving away from town all night. But there are so many of them, and even with the late additions, so few of us.

The more senior Riders look calm. I try to follow their lead. The air is colder in the cemetery, but the cool breeze is pleasant against my exertion-warmed muscles and the heat in my cheeks that keeps rising every time I catch Val's eye. Imani skips ahead on the playlist to "Another One Bites the Dust," which has all of us laughing at the irony and singing along. We Ride, confident and united, down the paths between graves, the barrier formed by the magic thrumming steadily as it slices through the crowd of ghosts around us and we replenish it from within.

My bike jerks under me. At first I think I must have hit a crack or a bump on the path, but the bike suddenly feels like it's being dragged along. I can tell from years of biking that the instability is coming from my back wheel. I risk a look back and see a formless glob of empty dark nothing threaded through the spokes, wrapping itself around the tire.

I try to scream, but terror clutches at my throat. I've never been this close to a ghost before. All the fear that had vanished in the warm light of the magic floods back into me. My bike slows and wobbles. The Ride pulls ahead. I try to yank my bike back upright, but the deflated back tire is sluggish to respond, and gravity pulls me down.

The momentum of the fall makes me roll away from my bike. My helmet whacks against something, probably a gravestone. I'm only dimly aware that a fall at that speed wasn't enough to injure me beyond stinging scrapes on my palms and elbows. The terror takes up all my attention. I can see nothing but a kind of darkness I never knew existed. This is the cemetery under a new moon. The ghosts around me blot out the stars in the sky and even the mediocre lights on my bike lying a few feet away. Freezing cold like I've never known pierces my skin, but I can't scream. The air around me is so thick with ghosts I'm afraid to breathe. It's not like the Ride would hear me over the music anyway.

Maybe it's better this way. This isn't a road near town like where we encountered the car. If the Ride were to stop here, the ghosts might overwhelm the music and the lights, just like the bonfires in the old days. Everyone would be in danger. The Ride doesn't need me, but I know that no matter how many streetlights they build, this town needs the Ride. Whatever the ghosts do to me, I'll be proud to say that I was a Rider once, even for half a night.

Then there's light, nearly blinding after a few seconds of nothing. It warms my skin and pierces the air all around me with its tiny, sparkling reflections off the glitter coating my cheeks. Maybe the glitter really *is* part of the magic—I need every photon I can get right now.

The Ride may not need me, but I showed up, and as they've shown me already over and over, that means they show up in return. They don't care what I look like or how well I know bikes or that I've never considered myself brave. They only care that I'm here.

The light is from Imani's bike, coming back toward me over the bumpy grass, followed by the rest of the Riders in single file behind her. I watch Imani turn into a curve, and then the magic stabilizes around me as the Ride coalesces into a crude circle, surrounding me and my fallen bike. The ghosts flee.

Apparently, my Ride isn't over.

Val glances anxiously at me, and I shoot her a thumbs up to reassure her I'm okay then gesture for her to stay in the circle. Mike has already peeled away to meet me in the center, swinging his backpack over one shoulder. "Flat tire?" he asks, shouting over the music.

"I think so," I shout back. I help Mike turn my bike upside down so that it rests on the handlebars and the basket in the back, the best we can do without the stands in the warehouse. Mike pulls the tire away from the rim and examines the tube, squinting in the darkness. I detach my front light—it's easy, now that I've watched the others install them—and hold it up so he can see better.

He finds the tear quickly. It's a rip so tiny I doubt I could have noticed it myself. "I can patch this," he says. "It should hold for the night."

The Ride continues in dizzying circles around us as I hold the tire still enough for Mike to apply the glue and patch. He replaces the tire and starts to refill it with a handheld pump until the man with the fancy mountain bike shouts something to us and tosses over a device that turns out to be a compressed gas tire inflator. It fills the tire in seconds. Mike squeezes it to make sure the patch will hold, then offers me back my bike.

I mount it without a second thought. The magic is still strong around us, but the ghosts are getting closer and denser the longer we stay still. No one really knows why the Ride works to keep the ghosts from their mischief so much better than anything else humans have tried, but as Imani finishes one last circle and pulls away down the path, the rest of us falling in behind her, I think I understand. The border between us, where our magic ends and the ghosts' begins, doesn't only belong to us Riders.

The ghosts don't retreat like they do from sunlight or hover outside like they do with the streetlights, they ride with us. They crave life, and we offer them a shining, shimmering pocket of it to bask in, joy and laughter and power and music to take back with them into the dark and the cold. And next month we'll do it again, because life comes in seasons and cycles, not permanent solutions like electric lights that make people forget when sunset is.

Val falls back to ride beside me again. I marvel at not needing to catch up to her at all—for once she slows down for me. She reaches toward me with one hand. She might just be planning to touch my arm again, to assure herself that I'm alive and okay, but I meet her in the middle and take her hand in mine. With each rotation of our tires, magic and power and life thrum through us as we ride into the darkness together, side by side.

DATE NIGHT

GRACE DESMARAIS

o o o
o o o
THAT'S YOUR COSTUME?
I WAS IN A RUSH.
PLUS, YOU'LL LOOK GOOD ENOUGH FOR THE BOTH OF US.
HOLD ON TIGHT, WE'VE GOT A LOT OF GROUND TO COVER TODAY. THE PARADE ALREADY STARTED.

HELL
RAISER

chu~

!
HA HA HA HA

HEY PRINCESS!
heh. nice.

HEH.
YOU CAN RIDE MY BIKE ANYTIME PRINCESS!

SAY THAT AGAIN...
SCUMBAG

NOT RIGHT NOW SWEETIE. THERE'S TOO MANY PEOPLE. LATER...

WHATEVER YOU WANT BABE.

Hours Later...
DID YOU HAVE FUN TODAY?
IT WAS PERFECT. EVERYONE HAD INCREDIBLE OUTFITS. INCLUDING YOU.

THE NIGHTS STILL YOUNG.

YOU LOOK PARTICULARLY SUSPICIOUS.

shrug~
HELL RAIS

WHERE'S OUR NEXT STOP?
AMITY PARK, NO MORE QUESTIONS THOUGH. I DON'T WANNA SPILL THE SURPRISE.

KEEP YOUR EYES CLOSED!
I AM!

THIS BETTER NOT BE ANOTHER CAMPING TRIP. YOU KNOW I HATE CAMPING, VI.

IT'S NOT. ALRIGHTY, OPEN.

MAE, MEET KEITH
AND TODD.

YOU DIDN'T HAVE TO VI.
OH, I DID.

HEY PRINCESS. YOUR HOT GIRLFRIEND SAID YOU NEEDED US FOR SOME FUN.
WHAT DO YOU SAY MAE? SHOULD WE HAVE SOME FUN? I EVEN BROUGHT YOUR FAVORITE TOY.
HELL RAISER
YOU KNOW ME SO WELL, BABE.
WHAT'S THAT FOR?
OH THIS? MEET
Francesca.
Francesca

francesca ♡
TWACK
CRACK
THNK
BEST.
DATE.
EVER.
the end

THE MIDNIGHT RIDE OF THE JACKAL ATTERN

ELLY BANGS

B left the state steelworks and K left the holy archives. Each threw careful glances over their shoulders now and then as they rode, watchful for any sign they were being followed; trying not to flinch whenever their satchels, heavy with occult contraband, banged against their sides with every crack in the asphalt. Their paths through the city united at a pre-arranged point, in the long October shadows of the skeletonized towers that still stood in what had been downtown. When K and B's distant but recognizable shapes were held securely in the corners of each other's visions, they pedaled onward without a word or a moment's pause. Studiously resisting eye contact, biting back any smile that began to form, keeping thirty feet apart so as to appear as strangers, they rode for miles—following the circuitous route described by a series of riddles, written in invisible ink on a square of toilet paper, recovered from a dead drop the night before—memorized and then flushed.

According to the lore of the infamous and despised followers of Attern, their heathen goddess traveled the universe on a bicycle carved out of ebony and bone—and had, through marvelous trickery, ridden her two creaky wheels to victory in a race against the God of the church-state in his golden chariot. For true believers like K, that story and all the others were the literal truth, and every turn of the crank was an act of devotion to her illegal faith. Atheists like B both heard and told those same stories as subversive jokes, no less wise and worthwhile for their absurdities: a bicycle was by far the smartest way to travel to a gathering of followers. No one would question them for cycling when fuel and electricity were being tightly rationed for the wars. A bicycle was quiet. It could fit through narrow passages. Above all, it kept a person moving slowly enough to notice the solutions to each riddle that pointed the secret way to their destination: a faded symbol drawn on the cracked pavement, a sticker on a stop sign, a place where the power lines aligned to carve a shape into the yellowing sky letting them know to turn down a narrow alley, into the safety of the shadows.

They risked the briefest glances at each other there and savored them hungrily before emerging back into the light.

They kept up a gentle pace, but with each block and turn their hearts pounded faster in growing awareness of the dangers they were riding into: maybe they hadn't decoded the message correctly, and they'd never find their way to the meeting place. Maybe they were being followed without knowing it, and they were even now leading the Knights of Purity straight to their targets. Maybe the message had been false and there was no secret gathering at all, only a trap, a whole brigade of Knights waiting to summarily cleanse anyone foolish and desperate enough to show up.

These fears burned most brightly when their route turned to follow the river south, and for a half-mile they rode directly alongside the Knights' barracks. Formations of men in dirty white and gold body armor marched down the asphalt just on the other side of the fence, their boot-clacks brutally synchronized, their automatic rifles gleaming in the red sunset. But the spotlights at the guard towers did not swivel to shine on the two passing cyclists, and the Knights all kept up their march. No one seemed to have any idea that the two unassuming passers-by, one in sooty work coveralls and the other in the uniform of a low cleric, were wicked unbelievers, criminal enemies of both church and state, on their way even now to practice the three occult rituals of their worship to a jackal-headed goddess: The Rite of Fear. The Rite of Darkness. The Rite of Death. An unholy trinity of pagan idolatry on this, a night whose name virtuous citizens of the Holy Confederacy would never dare to breathe aloud: Hollow Eve.

Thank Attern for shrouding us, K prayed under her breath as they cleared the barracks.

Thank our luck, B thought to herself.

When the last of the chain-link fence and razor wire receded into the sinking twilight and the rhythmic clack of bootheels was no longer audible, there was a moment of bodily relief. But as soon as fears of discovery and death had passed, new and sharper ones rushed in.

Maybe, B thought, K no longer felt about her the way she felt about K. And maybe, K thought, B wasn't quite the same person she remembered. Their romance was entering its third year but it had been a month since they'd been able to safely meet, not even to so much as sit on opposite sides of a public bench and exchange flirtatious notes behind their backs. A lot could change in a month.

And then, so suddenly, they realized they'd arrived. The last riddle had said '*Find us where the rain remembers the first and final shape of all things.*' Above the main entrance to a vast and crumbling warehouse at the end of the block, four sun-bleached plastic letters had fallen out of the word 'industries' but left a cutout of the word 'dust' painted on the concrete by dribbles of soot and lime. It was the perfect gathering place: this part of the city was long-abandoned for a half-mile in all directions, and there were numerous places to hide on approach to the front door.

B and K solemnly dismounted between two rusted shipping containers nearby. Only there did they dare to meet each other's eyes fully. They hugged tightly, once—long enough to feel the other's heart pounding, though they couldn't tell whether it pounded with fear or love. Each was afraid to ask.

They went to work shedding their costumes. B peeled away her sooty coveralls from a fitted black T-shirt with a low neckline; K wrestled out of her cleric's tunic and straightened the straps of the bright purple dress she wore beneath it. B slid her breast forms carefully into place while K adjusted her necklace and then cringed as she re-pierced her own ears with the sharpened tips of the hooks of her earrings. They applied makeup to each other's eyes, each stroke of pigment revealing the skin beneath it, just as the wigs they put on did not hide their heads, but rather exposed their truth. The close-cut scalps beneath were merely lies the two of them were forced to tell about themselves everywhere but here, always except for now. On Hollow Eve, between followers, there were no lies allowed.

"I missed you," K said.

"Always," B said. "So much."

They leaned closer as if to kiss, but hesitated too long. Instead they swallowed, drew back, and attended to the last details. They donned masks, mirrored and faceless and identical—not a lie but a self-censorship, as necessary for safety as for ritual. They walked the last distance and climbed a few ancient concrete steps to the open door. They hesitated, knowing it could still be a trap. Finally they held hands tightly and stepped through.

At first there was only musty darkness and the crunch of fallen paint and plaster under their soles. With each step, the muffled sound of conversation grew louder, the aroma of incense banished the mildew, and dim firelight guided them deeper, until they reached a large central chamber whose roof had long ago caved in, leaving it empty to the emerging stars. At the center of that space loomed the Jackal Attern, twenty feet tall, sharp ears, pointed snout, and all, with a commensurately huge bicycle at her side. Per tradition, the statue had been pasted together from dozens of pieces of cardboard and papier-mâché, each fashioned in secret and transported here separately. Under the Jackal's ever-vigilant eyes stood a thousand or more of her followers in their mirrored masks: conversing in whispers, greeting lovers and strangers and long-lost friends alike, basking in the communal warmth—or giddily searching for enthusiastic partners in the impending Rite of Darkness. K and B realized they had arrived just in time: a hush spread through the crowd as the High Priest approached the statue and raised his arms to it in supplication, the motion spreading the sides of his cloak like wings. The fabric was plain black linen at first glance, but the firelight reflected intricate patterns of subtle embroidery: countless shapes and colors hiding in the dark. Only when the silence was perfect did he turn to face the gathering.

His was the only unmasked face in the room. Every Hollow Eve, B searched that face instinctively for any sign of fear at his exposure. All she ever saw was a grounded calm she envied beyond words.

"We are who we are," he said. "We come here to unite in a siblinghood, ancient and eternal, shared by everyone who is or has ever been who they are not supposed to be."

His voice was low, but it carried impossibly well, amplified by the acoustics of the space, B thought; by some marvelous magic, K believed. No one could do anything but listen.

"The dead, also, are here with us tonight," he continued, drawing a brief chorus of muted sobs. "Some who were here with us as flesh and bone only last year. Others in generations stretched back to the beginning of time. They come to join us in celebration that we still live. In the way of the Jackal, camouflage, trickery, quiet, and nimble speed have kept you hidden and safe in the shadows, and your wheels have spun true to return you here. Another year has passed, and your hearts are still here, beating. Your survival has completed the Rite of Fear."

B and K let out breaths they'd forgotten they were holding, and similar exhales sounded from everyone around them. In this place they stood shoulder-to-shoulder with heretics and subversives. Scientists and philosophers. Librarians who hoarded books they were supposed to burn and historians who remembered what they were supposed to forget. Women who excelled in any of the ten thousand skills that were supposed to be the sole domain of men. Doctors who offered life-saving care when they were supposed to turn their patients in for so much as asking for it. Artists and musicians whose secret works mocked or simply ignored the church-state that their skills were supposed to exclusively exalt. Alongside them stood husbands who were supposed to have wives; daughters who were supposed to be sons; people who were supposed to be either men or women, but who were both or neither. Some of Attern's followers believed in her with religious passion while others were consummate atheists who'd only come for the party, and they were equally welcome. Behind all their mirrored masks, those present were all, in their own ways, survivors who were supposed to be dead.

"And so we begin the Rite of Darkness," the High Priest said.

A wave of giddy energy washed through the crowd. The impatient and impious were already hurrying away into the halls and small rooms off the central chamber. K and B stayed to listen, their pulses thundering in their ears, their unspoken fears rising again with the High Priest's voice.

"All shadows everywhere are the Jackal's kingdom. A sanctuary to which she welcomes each of us in our times of need. We do not cease to be who we are simply because we are unseen, and we do not need our eyes to know each other. In the dark, sight has no lies left to tell. It is in the dark that we know each other best."

There was plenty of time for each participating pair or group to find their own place in the building, as secluded or open as they wished. B joined the crowd and led K along, nearly stumbling in fear that after all of this her lover would let go of her hand. K was acutely aware of every microscopic hesitation in B's body ahead of her, and she trembled with worry at the rejection each one might foretell. But they reached an empty room, with stalactites of lime on the walls, a guttering lamp in the corner, and a crude, straw-packed bedroll on the floor. They faced each other and the sweat pooled between their palms until K finally reached to extinguish the lamp. The long-awaited darkness finally arrived, curling like smoke into every corner of the building, until everywhere but the central chamber was pitch-black.

Many followers contented themselves to chastely loiter and converse there by the statue of Attern, but they kept their mirrored masks on. It was only in the lightless spaces that B and K and many hundreds of others—their queer or simply non-procreative love labeled as illegal and satanic outside these walls—reached eagerly behind their heads, undid the knotted strings, and let their naked faces feel the cool air without worry of being seen or identified by informants.

There was always an explosion of laughter and noise in those first minutes of the Rite of Darkness, when its participants inevitably crashed into each other and fell across the floor in their long-awaited frenzy to finally touch each other: arms to backs of necks, tongues to tongues, hands to zippers and waistbands and belts and everything beneath. But K and B took it slow, at first. Their lips tasted the salt of each others' unseeing eyes, felt the warmth of each other's fast and shaky breaths, and finally made wandering paths across each other's necks and then faces, until finally they found each other.

When they'd had all they could stand, they lay together, listening to each other breathe.

"Do you believe in the Jackal?" K asked. "In all this time, we've never really talked about it."

B chuckled, "Of course not." She hesitated and asked nervously, "I mean . . . do you?"

"I do." K gave B's face a gentle stroke to let her know she wasn't offended. "Why don't you?"

B considered this for a moment.

"I spend all day stamping crucifixes into gun barrels because the Pastor General thinks it makes the bullets fly miraculously true," she answered. "It's not working on the Illinois front, is it? And how many of Attern's followers didn't make it back this year? How many of them needed a miracle that never came? I see no miracles in this world."

"You don't believe in miracles because they're not *reliable?*" K chided. "If they were, they'd be called something else."

"Way I see it, if something can't be proved, it's imaginary nonsense. I've always figured Attern worship is just a hodgepodge of stuff our grandparents' generation misremembered, our parents' generation misheard, our generation misinterpreted. If Hollow Eve was even a thing a hundred years ago, it was probably really different."

"It was," K conceded.

B turned on her side to face her, head resting on her arm. "Really?"

K laughed. "I work in the archives, remember? Sometimes they leave me alone with old books on their way to the furnace, so I read. People have been celebrating Hollow Eve for centuries, but it was nothing like this before the Holy Confederacy outlawed it. It used to be playful, unserious. The only rites were dressing up as fictional characters and giving candy to children."

"But they still worshipped Attern?"

K shook her head. "No. Attern bears some interesting similarities to a very old god called Anubis, who guided people through the underworld and weighed their souls on a scale, but we've only been worshipping Attern for fifty years. She's, um . . ." K sighed. She dearly wanted B to at least respect her faith, and this wasn't going to help, but tonight was supposed to be in part a celebration of the full truth. "Listen, just . . . don't laugh. Okay?"

B braced herself and nodded. "Okay."

"So, before the Confederacy, there was this Hollow Eve tradition where people would carve out a big squash and then cut a face into it. And they called that squash a Jackalattern."

B was glad K couldn't see her expression. She managed not to laugh. "So we're all here tonight to worship a goddess who's named after . . . a vegetable with a face."

"I'm afraid so."

"Huh." B pressed every trace of amusement out of her voice. "So that's why it's called Hollow Eve—because that's when you hollow out the gourd?"

"Nope."

K said this so simply and so seriously that, after a tense pause, neither could hold back a breathless fit of laughter.

"But you *still* believe in Attern?" B asked, when she could. "I didn't think you cared for this stuff any more than me. You told me the Confederate Bible is the same way. Revised, cut up, rewritten, some parts forgotten, and other parts emphasized to suit someone's politics. How is this any different?"

"I told you I don't believe what the church teaches about purity and conquest, but that doesn't mean I don't know the power of faith," K said. "It's supernatural in its own right. Wonderful and terrible things happen any time people join together to *believe* something. That's what makes it so important to choose carefully and thoughtfully—choose who and what to believe in."

"Even if it's false?"

"Not everything that can't be proved is false."

K's hand went to the necklace she wore: a tiny silver sprocket, tarnished nearly black.

"But you're saying you *chose* to believe in Attern," B said. "You didn't witness some miracle that proved to you that She's real. You could've picked any illegal deity from any forbidden religious text in the archive, and you chose this one? She has the best rituals, that's for sure."

K chuckled, but then turned solemn. "What does it mean to you that Her symbol is a bicycle?"

After a moment's thought, B shrugged. "Quick and quiet and nimble. Good for staying inconspicuous."

"I'll tell you what it means to me." K guided B's hand to the necklace and let her fingertips feel its tiny sprocket teeth. "The church-state knows it's Her sacred symbol–ours–but they can't outlaw bikes. They're already everywhere. And they're everywhere because they don't need the fuel nobody can get, or the parts nobody can afford, or the hours nobody has to spend fixing them when they die. With a bike, as long as you've got two legs and an eye you can keep moving. If the chain breaks you push with your feet. If the tires pop you patch them or you ride on the bare rims until the spokes all snap. Just think of everything that went wrong with Attern's bicycle when She raced against God in His chariot, and still She won!"

She knew she'd let her voice get too loud. She took a breath and finished, "That's why every day I choose again to believe in Her. Because to keep living, I need to believe hope works like that. And I choose to keep living."

B stared into the part of the darkness where she knew K lay next to her and felt a buoyant warmth rise through her chest. She was certain she'd never share K's faith, not even a fraction of it. Maybe she'd never even manage not to find it partly absurd. But she was surprised to realize that she also found it dazzlingly beautiful.

"I love you," B said, without thinking.

Even in the pitch black, K was sure she could somehow feel the way B was looking at her: adoring, breathless, insatiable.

"I love you, too."

They held each other's faces and pulled closer—but just then a low, quiet bell sounded, moving down the corridor outside, letting everyone know to re-tie their mirrored masks and grope around for their discarded clothes. Minutes later, the bell would be followed by a flame, and the darkness would gently surrender to the spreading warmth of thousands of candles. No matter how much they ached at having to hide their faces from each other again, it was time for the final rite.

“We could skip the rest,” B said. “We could keep the light out and stay right here.”

K lay her hand on the top of B’s chest and took a slow breath, drawing up the will to resist the temptation. The Rites meant everything to her. B sighed and nodded, and they dressed, tied their masks on, and walked back to the central chamber.

“And so we begin the Rite of Death,” said the High Priest.

Throughout the space, dozens of sheets were pulled to unveil illegal drawings, paintings, and sculptures. Musicians and their instruments emerged from the crowd and set up at Attern’s massive cardboard feet to play outlawed songs for forbidden dances. Meanwhile, everyone reached into bags and backpacks and pockets and drew out their sacred offerings to each other: little misshapen cookies, flat pastries with dried fruit, sticks covered in glittering jewels of crystallized sugar. The only traditional requirements for a Tricker Treat were that it be about the size of a fist and tooth-achingly sweet—as sweet as the triumph of surviving another year through care and cunning.

K reached into her satchel, but B had beat her to it. K took the Treat from her lover’s cupped hands and unwrapped it—first with meticulous care, and then with an astonishment that was visible in her hands alone.

“You *baked* this,” K said, tearing off a piece of the ring-shaped cake and feeling its unmistakable spongy texture between her fingers. “With real cricketflour and everything? How? With all the rationing . . .”

B’s face glowed with pride. “I found a spot behind one of the furnaces where it’s always just about hot enough. But it’s not cricket. It’s *wheat*. It’s got a real chicken egg in it, too.”

They looked at each other: K struggling to mentally calculate what a fortune those ingredients must have cost; B savoring the delighted disbelief in her lover’s body language. B would remember it for the whole year ahead, and that memory was worth twice what it had cost her. But then K huffed in frustration.

B put her hands up. “Hey, the rationing is really harsh right now. You know I won’t be hurt if you couldn’t get . . .”

K shoved a small bundle of colorful plastic at B. Inside was a bar of chocolate wrapped in foil that shone like solid gold in the firelight. B broke off a piece and slipped it carefully beneath the bottom of her mask. She closed her eyes and moaned in disbelief.

"This is real chocolate," B said. "How did you get real chocolate?!"

K shook her head bitterly. "It took me eight months to find a source and arrange the barter. I *really* thought this was going to be the year I finally one-upped you."

They walked hand-in-hand around through the crowd, slipping bite after bite under their masks and savoring each taste even after the sweetness became intolerable. They took in each work of art and note of music with that same determined hunger, trying to tattoo every sound and image and sensation of touch onto their brains. That same desperation gradually stiffened the spines of everyone around them, and the mood turned jagged as the followers of Attern sensed the night drawing to its close.

The musicians finished their final song and set down their instruments, and the last dancers went still. Then the artists, in solemn motions that hurt to watch, gathered up all their masterworks and piled them at the feet of the statue of Attern, while every participant in the Rite of Darkness layered their bedrolls on top, and the High Priest walked a slow circle of the heap, pouring out a libation of gasoline.

There was no avoiding this. Reports of strange music would bring Knights here sooner or later, and fingerprints and DNA traces found their way into everything. Still, everyone's eyes began to water under their masks, even before the first wisps of smoke rose from the heap.

The High Priest turned to face the silent crowd. His silhouette darkened into a void as the flames behind him brightened. He raised his voice above the snaps of burning wood to say, "Church and state have always tried to stamp us out, and they have always failed. And even could they quench every last living spark of us, still our fire would catch, again and again—from nothing, if it must."

B and K, and soon everyone around them, held hands tightly as the fire ate up the crude cardboard and plaster hulk of Attern herself. The Goddess of trickery and broken rules, K thought; the saint of the shadows that keep prey safely hidden from their predators; the spirit that guards all beautiful secrets and preserves the people who must keep them.

The made-up deity of vegetables with funny faces, B thought, biting the smile from her lips.

"The Rite of Death is completed and the Rite of Fear begins again," said the High Priest. "For another year, we don our costumes. May the Jackal ride alongside you and offer you shade in all the bright places through which you must travel, until we can all come home to each other again."

The followers one by one turned away from the pyre and dissolved back into the night, jaws set and fists clenched. The musicians resigned themselves to a year of silence. The wise steeled themselves for another year of feigned ignorance. And while the other women braced to hide again under the bulky costumes of submission and docility, K and B struggled to remember how to pretend to be men. It was a skill they'd honed all their lives, but in only these few short hours it felt as if it had rusted away into nothing.

The meeting place was becoming more dangerous now by the second as the smoke rose higher into the sky above them, but still B and K hesitated. They stood there caressing each other's arms until all but a few others had gone, watching the statue become unrecognizable and finally collapse.

"If She *were* to exist," B asked, "do you think She'd be miffed at me for knowing She doesn't?" She hoped it sounded as joking as she meant it.

"Probably not," K replied, hoping she didn't sound as serious as she felt.

With bone-deep reluctance they turned their back on the embers and walked out into the night. In the space between the shipping containers, by the lights of their bicycles' headlights, they changed back into their costumes: B re-wrapping herself in the coveralls of a workman of the state steelworks; K hiding her necklace and shrouding her bright purple dress in the gray tunic of a clerical officer of the holy archives. They tucked their wigs back into their satchels and carefully wiped every trace of makeup from each others' faces. They took a few minutes to study a map and plan their routes home; by now a full curfew would be in effect, and only the lightless and abandoned streets would be safe. They shared one last long, deep kiss, and then they mounted their bicycles and rode—instinctively keeping thirty feet apart, holding each other firmly in the corners of their visions but never making eye contact. B inwardly counted down the blocks before their paths through the city would have to diverge.

Later, she would curse herself for that. If only she'd been a little less lovestruck, she might have kept a better lookout for a flicker of light or whisper of motion around the next corner. She might have noticed the patrol car before its bank of spotlights flared to white-hot life, stopping B and K in their tracks.

"Stop!" a lone Knight barked, thunderously loud. He whipped his rifle off his shoulder. "You're in violation of curfew. What are you doing in this zone?"

K began, "Me? I was—"

"This is a zone of suspected unholy and criminal activity," he interrupted. "Drop your bicycles and bags. On your knees. Now! Hands behind your heads!"

The urge to comply without thinking was strong and ingrained. Nothing about this was unusual. Except . . .

Except tonight their satchels contained mirrored masks. Crumbs of Tricker Treat. Wigs, makeup, breasts. If he searched them, they were dead.

K looked directly at B, and each knew exactly what the other was thinking.

Don't, B pleaded with her eyes.

No choice, K replied with hers—because what had her faith and its sacred lore prepared her for better than this? Attern on Her bicycle had raced against the God of the church-state in His gleaming chariot, and won.

They stomped on their pedals and swerved around, shooting away from those burning lights. B swore under her breath while K whispered frantic prayers. Only fifty feet ahead there was an alley too narrow for the Knight's car to follow them through. It only had to lead to another street the Knights hadn't blocked off, or to a half-collapsed building with ample hiding places. They only needed to cross that shrinking distance. Twenty more feet. Ten.

The shot rang out and K yelped, then fell at the edge of the spotlights' reach. Her bicycle's rear tire was deflated and the wheel had snapped apart. B realized that was where the bullet had hit. She could see there was no trace of blood or sign of a wound, but K wasn't moving.

B half-fell off her bicycle and ran to her love. In some corner of her mind she was aware that this was her last chance to escape, and she knew escape was exactly what K would want for her, but it made no difference. She couldn't leave. She could only kneel there, cradling K's head and trying to shut out the snap of the Knight's boots against the pavement behind her, his commands to raise her hands, the rattle of the handcuffs he drew from his belt. She'd imagined a moment like this one so many times, and she had always known she wouldn't spend the bitter end of her life cowering in fear or flinching away from some Knight's shouted threats.

She would spend it loving K. Her impossible beauty. Her limitless kindness. Her will. Her faith. And in that thought, she heard herself whisper: *May Attern shroud us.*

B paused. She almost laughed, despite it all—to find herself here, praying to an imaginary Goddess of gourds. But this was no time for dignity.

Fuck it, she thought.

"Attern," she whispered. "Attern who rules the night and the shadows, shroud and protect us. Deliver us from this deadly light."

"Final warning!" the Knight bellowed.

B looked up at him and saw how he seemed to burn in the spotlights, a white flame against the dark street behind him.

An electric tingle came to the back of her neck. A suffocating tension gathered in the night air. The old brick buildings pulled in tighter and then disappeared when the patrol car's bank of spotlights flickered and went out.

Then there was only terror and adrenaline. Impossible motion. Instinct and flight.

They were nearly a mile away by the time B could think clearly again. She was out of breath. Her muscles burned and her bicycle's rusty spokes creaked under the weight of K's dazed form hunching unsteadily on the back rack, feet braced against the chainstays, arms wrapped around B's waist.

"What happened?" K murmured, drowsily. Her head ached terribly where she'd hit the pavement. "Did we . . . get away?"

A few more blocks passed before B found the voice to answer, "Yes."

"How? You . . . fought that Knight?"

B grasped for the words to tell her what had happened. To describe how, when the spotlight had gone out, the blackness that had rushed in had even blotted out the stars.

How the Knight had swung around to face it, sweeping his rifle around in frantic motions to probe that void with the flashlight mounted on the barrel. The darkness had eaten up the beam like an infinite, empty distance.

How two massive eyes had opened above their heads and looked down, hollow and backlit with tongues of orange flame. Ears like swords swiveled in ceaseless vigilance. A long snout hinged open and bared teeth as sharp and white as the crescent moon B could no longer see.

The clawed fingers that closed around the Knight's body made him look as small as a Tricker Treat—and then he was simply gone like smoke on the wind. When those firelit eyes locked onto B, she had no breath to scream. Her pulse hammered on her eardrums and her body felt encased in cement. The Jackal Attern, Goddess of Shadows, Guardian of Secrets, stared down at her and sniffed.

Appraising, B thought. Judging. Weighing her soul on a scale and deciding whether to whisk her away into the very same nothingness.

After a moment's pause, the Goddess let out a short, high cry, all too like a laugh. Then She turned and rode away into the night on a bicycle carved out of ebony and bone.

It wasn't B's lack of any proof, or her pride, that choked her voice off every time she opened her mouth to tell K any of this. It was fear of the inadequacy of language to describe it: a marrow-deep sense that the night itself might overhear her tale and find it lacking.

"Just . . . hold on," B said, finally. "I'll get you home safe."

She rode on through the midnight streets, whispering prayers under her breath, and carefully dodging out of the reach of every street lamp, keeping always in the shadows.

First Date Jitters

Kortney Nash

Moni kicks the nearest trash can in agitation, reeling back in pain when she remembers it's pure steel and bolted to the ground. The park is quiet, save for her muttered curses and heavy breathing while she alternates between boxing the air and reaching for the white-hot agony radiating from her foot. It's just before dusk—the youngest trick-or-treaters are still wrapping up their rounds before the older kids come out in their *Scream* masks to take candy by the handful from frazzled homeowners. None of that registers as she bowls in half, drawing on meditative prowess she doesn't possess to will the hurt away. She's keeled over like that, clutching her throbbing foot with a fury so intense it's left her mute, when she's approached by the girl she was agonizing over in the first place.

"Are you okay?" a soft voice asks, while maintaining a cautious distance. When Moni looks up the girl is eying her warily from two arms lengths away, unsubtly clutching the strap of her tote bag in a death grip. She's wearing oversized jeans and a tube top with a bent pair of cat ears stuck haphazardly on top of her headwrap. Even through her obvious caution, there's a genuine concern in her eyes that warms Moni from the inside out.

Moni offers a smile, one that she hopes is disarming enough to belie the slowly dissipating discomfort from her affected foot. "I like your cat costume."

"There's not really much to it." The girl raises an amused eyebrow. "Was that you who screamed earlier?"

"Screamed?"

"Someone, or something, screamed out like they were dying."

"Must've been someone else." Moni shrugs, leaning closer to test the waters. Then even closer when the girl doesn't move to step back. "There are lots of weirdos in this area . . ." She ignores the surrounding debris-less sidewalks and manicured lawns that telegraph micromanaged suburbia. "You should let me escort you home. For safety or whatever."

The girl laughs, a musical sound with a slight edge that only makes Moni even more interested. "You're very forward."

"Do you like it?"

"I don't hate it," she responds, her face settling into a barely-there smile. "I'm Ada."

Moni had already known her name but doesn't say as much, instead introducing herself with a wink that she hopes lands. For a breathless moment they just hold eye contact, both waiting for the other to do something. Moni lets herself study Ada's face unabashedly, from wide brown eyes to the sharp cupid's bow of her lips—Moni hadn't met many other girls before, but it was easy for her to to decide Ada was the most perfect girl, that something had peaked in the universe when she was born and now Moni was fortunate enough to behold this modern miracle of a woman.

Finally, Moni's face splits into a smirk, even as she shyly averts her gaze. "So, you gonna let me take you out to eat?"

"You really don't waste any time," Ada laughs once more. "Sure, I'll let you take me to get some food. I'm starving."

Moni nods, willing the blush creeping up her neck to subside. She can feel herself burning up under her ridiculously large pink faux fur coat—she's dressed as the rapper Cam'ron for Halloween, fake flip phone and all. "I can take us somewhere on my bike."

"Fancy," Ada deadpans, following Moni to the parking lot. Then, minutes later, "Oh, you meant a *bike* bike. Like a bicycle."

"C'mon, don't say it like that. This is a fourth-generation Cyclowheel mountain bike. I swear to God the ride is smoother than most cars." Moni swings a leg over the seat. "You can stand on the pegs and hold my shoulders." When Ada hesitates she continues. "I'm a strong rider, seriously. And there's a diner only like five blocks away . . . I really wanna share a milkshake with you."

Ada rolls her eyes but takes a wobbly step onto the pegs. Moni basks in the familiar feeling of Ada gripping her shoulders, tapering her giddiness with a deep, steadying breath.

"Have you done this before?" Ada's voice is laced with barely concealed worry as Moni jerkily peels out of the parking lot.

"Done what? Rode with a really pretty girl on the back of my bike? I'm afraid this is the first time, it's super sad when you think about it."

"Moni."

"Trust me, I won't let anything happen to us. The Cyclowheel was made to be enjoyed with others." Moni lifts a hand from her handlebar to wave away Ada's concern but quickly sets it down when they teeter precariously. She rides in the street, nearly in the gutter; tiny trick-or-treaters waddling by on the sidewalk to her right while minivans lurch by on her left, the sun nearly setting behind them on the horizon. Moni wishes she could trap this moment in a bottle, greedily wants to covet the feeling of Ada's hands simply resting on her shoulders as a light breeze carries the scent of something being grilled just out of sight.

They arrive at the diner all too soon and not soon enough. Obnoxious Halloween-themed decorations line every surface: gauzy spider web covering the walls and plastic jack-o'-lanterns sitting on every table. It's crowded, full of people in generic costumes contributing to a steady undercurrent of white noise that tangles with the staticky rendition of "Monster Mash" spilling from a worn down jukebox in the corner.

"This is my favorite spot." It's the only spot Moni knows, really. She leads Ada to a booth in the back without waiting for the host to turn his attention to them. "And now I'm here with my favorite girl."

Ada's smile wavers as she slides into her seat across the table. "We don't even really know each other yet."

"Sorry, I just . . . I can lay it on thick sometimes, sorry." Moni plays with the fraying edge of her T-shirt, chanting *Don't fuck this up again* in her head until she's nearly numb with it.

"So . . ." Ada lets her eyes drift around the room, the brown of her irises so dark they remind Moni of black coffee. Dark enough for her to see her own reflection in, the worry line creasing her forehead and the tense set of her shoulders. Moni makes a conscious decision to exhale and relax.

"What were you doing in the park earlier?" Ada asks, dragging a manicured finger across the surface of the table, making idle patterns.

"I was talking with a . . . friend, but she left right before you showed up." Then, because she can't help it, "It looks like it all worked out for the best though."

"Were you guys fighting? You looked angry."

"No, well . . . she hurt my feelings, but it's water under the bridge. What were *you* doing in the park?" Moni counters, turning to thank the waitress when menus are set down in front of them.

"I was . . ." Ada's brow furrows, something troubled passing over her expression before vanishing as quickly as it appeared. "Sorry, I couldn't remember for a second. I tutor kids at the library on Wednesdays. I was on my way home." Moni can see the memory weaving itself into existence as Ada speaks, filling in what was undoubtedly a smooth, blank plane in her mind. It's sometimes better this way, letting Ada's subconscious rationalize and mend the gaps in her memory. Usually buys some time before everything comes rushing back to her all at once.

"Cute, what do you do during the rest of the week?"

"I'm in school to become a software engineer." Ada smiles brightly at this. "I graduate this year, actually, just one more project to finish until I'm all done. Are you also at the local uni?"

"I wish," Moni offers without elaborating. She'd lied about attending uni in her past dates with Ada and it had only complicated things. Ruined them, really. "Software engineering sounds hard, I understand why you didn't have time to wear a real costume today."

"All the kids at the library loved my cat ears. Not really sure Cam'ron on a bike would've struck the same chord with them."

"All I really care about is whether it strikes a chord with you."

Ada's responding grin speaks a thousand words. "I'm here, aren't I? Besides, I've been having this huge Y2K phase recently. I'm into everything retro."

"Me too, it's why I love my bike so much—the Cyclowheel mountain series draws on a timeless nostalgia from the late twentieth century while utilizing contemporary safety features . . ." Moni starts, cutting herself off when the waitress from earlier reappears with a pen and pad, gaze expectant. "Is it okay if I order for both of us?"

"You don't even know whether I have any food allergies."

"Do you have any food allergies?"

" . . . no."

Moni rolls her eyes before ordering them one large milkshake and two sets of fries. She'd ordered them every milkshake on the menu before, and Ada always responded most favorably to Oreo-flavored with extra whipped cream sans the cherry on top. The one time Moni had ordered the banana cream shake Ada had made up some excuse and left after a single sip.

"So, is Moni short for anything?" Ada asks once the waitress leaves.

"Some say it's short for Monster," Moni bares her teeth in jest, "but it *may* just be short for Monroe."

"I've always loved the name Monroe," Ada gasps, something giddy appearing in her expression. "It's so pretty, it's been my favorite since I was a kid."

"What about you? What's 'Ada' short for?" Moni asks, not for the first time.

"Nothing at all. I'm just Ada."

I know, Moni thought, *that's what makes you so special.*

Their bill is on the house. Ada thanks the staff profusely while Moni drags her out, before she can notice how repetitive everyone's responses are. Being back outside is a welcome relief, another hurdle passed for the time being.

"There's still a bit of daylight left, is it okay if I take you somewhere cool? Somewhere with a view?" Moni asks, wringing her hands and then smoothing them out at her sides.

Ada pauses before responding, surveying the dregs of early evening light still painting the sidewalks golden. "This might sound weird, but it feels like it should be dark already, don't you think?"

"It hasn't been that long." Moni brushes her off, side-stepping an infant dressed as a ladybug. "If we leave now, we might make it in time to properly watch the sunset."

"I . . . yeah, okay," Ada concedes, confusion evident on her face. Moni knows they won't have much longer together, and pedals extra fast to draw it out just a little more. She's become used to this, milking the euphoria of each first date dry before it's even ended. Always, always, always racing against the inevitable moment when Ada finally remembers everything.

Moni's brought them back to the park; she leaves the bike in the lot and leads Ada by the hand up the tallest hill in the sprawling fields of grass. Tall enough for them to watch the vibrant rays of a never-setting sun dance across the eerily geometric housing community spanning as far as the eye can see.

"It's pretty, right? You know I could've gotten us here on my bike—the wheels are effective on grass and gravel as well as pavement—but I've learned the walk is nicer." Moni rambles, Ada's hand still in her own.

"You're really into biking," Ada comments through a giggle, taking a breathless seat on the plush grass as Moni does the same.

"M'not really into biking in general, just into my fourth generation Cyclowheel mountain bike specifically. It's built to BMX industry standards but priced affordably enough for the average consumer." Moni can't help the pre-programmed response spilling out of her mouth. Hasn't been able to help it no matter how much she's tried to stifle the innate urge to spit out fact after fact about the indomitable Cyclowheel.

"That's . . . really nice." Ada's laugh is more strained as she removes her hand from Moni's and places it in her own lap.

"Do you . . . do you like biking, too?"

"Not especially. I think my senior project had something to do with biking though, but I . . . I can't really remember. Maybe I haven't been getting enough sleep; my mind feels super hazy."

"We should've gotten you coffee at the diner."

"I don't think that would've been as romantic as sharing a milkshake."

"So, you admit it was romantic?" Moni attempts, and ultimately fails, to stop the excitement from bleeding into her voice.

"A little." Ada hedges. "Do you bring all of your dates here?"

"Only the ones I really really really like." Moni's gaze shifts to the grass squished between her fingers. "That means only you, by the way."

"I feel so special."

"You make me feel special, too, so I guess we're even?"

"I guess so." With Moni's earlier social faux paus already in the past they've moved closer again, really close. Nearly nose-to-nose. Moni's heartbeat thunders a desperate rhythm in her chest with each second that elapses. She'd only been able to kiss Ada on 27% of their first dates. Ada remembered everything too soon for them to even make it out of the diner most of the time.

Moni leans in to close the gap but is halted by Ada's hand gently pushing her away.

"Sorry, sorry, it's just . . . the sun seriously isn't setting, have you noticed that?" Ada gestures at the muted gold tones still setting the block alight, frowning. "I can't be the only one who thinks this is strange?"

"I'm sure it's moved a little, it's just slow is all—a watched kettle never boils, right?" Moni tries to laugh it off, tries to recreate the mood from earlier but Ada is already standing.

"No, something's not right here. I . . ." She brings her hands to her temples with a hiss. "This is . . ."

Moni already knows what's coming before Ada says it. Can see the recognition, horror, and anger flooding her expression as her eyes go from warm to accusatory in less than a second.

"This isn't real," she gasps, taking several steps back in quick succession and almost tripping over herself. "You . . . You're . . ."

"Monroe the Mountain Bike expert," Moni finishes with a resigned sigh. "The mascot you designed for the immersive virtual reality Cyclowheel Halloween ad campaign experience. Your senior thesis."

"Holy shit, I . . . how many times have we done this now?" Ada's eyes are blown wide as she does a full 360, taking in the neat world she'd coded herself whilst hunched over her laptop in a long series of sleepless nights, urged on by the thought of finally graduating. "You've *trapped* me here—in this unfinished simulation. You've been doing this over and over."

"I like you a lot."

"You're not *real*," Ada cries out in disbelief. "You're just rows of binary, I . . . you're only meant to take the consumer on a bike ride around town and relay the highlights of the fourth gen. I made you myself—I made all of this myself, it's not even *done* yet. I haven't even finished coding the trajectory of the sunset and the passage of time. I never even finished coding *you*—you're a terrible bike rider, I need to reset your center of gravity."

"You coded me enough to feel, to love. To experience joy and yearning, too. You coded me to feel pain and that's as real as it gets, can't you see that?" Moni reaches for Ada's hand but flinches when it's yanked away violently. "*Please*, I know we could be happy together, I just need you to stay here. It's lonely without you. I can't let you leave me—I'm sorry, please just give me a chance. Give *us* a chance, we can both be happy here." She's grown used to begging for Ada's love, for Ada's mercy, for anything Ada can give that's not outright rejection and disgust. But it never works.

Moni still regards her early days of existence spent without Ada with visceral terror. She was the only sentient avatar in the simulation, made to interact fluidly with users and charm them with a bike ride through the cozy autumnal suburb. The rest of the world was populated with underdeveloped characters who were only programmed to deliver a limited number of subpar, canned responses. Moni had been losing her *mind* before Ada initially visited to test the software. It was the first time she'd met someone else who could hold a conversation, who also had thoughts and dreams and opinions and who laughed and frowned and all these other minute things that screamed she was *alive*. Then Ada had left to go back to the real world and Moni swore if Ada ever returned, she would never, ever let her leave again.

"I have a life, an *actual* life—how long have I even been in here? How many times has the simulation restarted?" Ada sounds like she's on the verge of hyperventilating, a trembling hand brought to her heart. "How are you even doing this? You shouldn't be able to do this. Were we hacked? Is someone controlling the whole program remotely?"

Moni doesn't tell Ada that this is their 105th first date. Nor does she explain the intricacy of how all of Ada's sleepless nights had resulted in corrupted code, a foothold that Moni had used to wiggle her digital consciousness into the fabric of the entire virtual world. That this flaw allowed her to overwrite the automatic wake-up trigger that was meant to pulse to the electrodes attached to Ada's temples in the real world where she's presently in a deep, medicated sleep.

"It'll be so much better if you stop fighting me, I promise, really." Moni clasps her hands in front of her in a pleading gesture. "You had fun today, right? Just you and me and the fourth generation Cyclowheel mountain bike that comes with a free ten-year warranty and a set of 12-speed replacement chains. Everyday could be like this, just us hanging out and riding around the neighborhood. Wouldn't that be fun? Wouldn't that be . . ."

Ada screams, falling to her knees and cradling her head in her hands. "You need to let me out of here, this is *insane!*"

"I can't, Ada, I can't. I'm sorry, but I can't. Not unless you can take me with you."

"I can't take you with me because you're not real. You're not real, *you're not real.* I . . . Oh my God, I was by myself when I hooked myself up to the program. I was only supposed to be in here for five minutes," Ada says wetly. "I don't know how long it'll take for anyone to find me."

"You don't have to worry about any of that, it doesn't matter anymore." Moni squats in front of her. "None of that matters anymore."

"Get away from me," Ada spits out, scooting backwards and rising to unsteady feet. "You *monster*." She swallows the rest of her words before turning around and stomping down the hill.

"Where are you going?" Moni calls, running after her.

"Stay *away* from me," Ada shouts, "I don't want to see you ever again, I'm finding a way out of here." She picks up her pace, crossing the grass and parking lot in sharp, determined strides while Moni watches from the base of the hill.

In fifty-one of their dates, Ada crossed the street without looking and was struck by a minivan that was not coded to watch out for pedestrians. Moni soon finds out this is another one of those, the thud echoing loudly in the otherwise preternaturally quiet block before Moni can even cry out for her to stop.

Moni howls in anguish, slamming her foot into the nearest trash can and then gasping in pain. She'd fucked it again, the failure a heavy weight on her soul. That's how Ada finds her for the 106th time, after the 106th respawn: crouched over in agony while she breathes through the pain. There's a concerned frown on the other girl's face as she asks if everything is okay.

"Now that you're here everything is more than fine," Moni replies, the tension already seeping from her body. Sometimes Ada remembers everything shortly after respawning, other times Moni is blessed with long, uninterrupted hours of Ada's laughter and banter before some innocuous detail triggers everything to come back to her. There's no telling what this time will bring, but Moni smiles nonetheless. She takes a deep breath, ready to try again.

"Are you busy? I'd love to take you out for dinner, we can ride together on my bike."

Unfinished Business

Valerie Hunter

In the second week of October, Emma had to display the pumpkins in the front window of SaveMart. The pumpkins in question were pitiful looking—grungy, lumpy, possibly fungus-infected—but Emma shoved them onto the shelves dutifully because that's what she'd been told to do. Over a year into her employment she was still only part-time because none of the full-time people ever quit or retired. Apparently a full-time job at SaveMart was a pot of gold you had to hold onto, which Emma found too depressing to contemplate. The current full-timers' ages ranged from mid-twenties to early seventies, but they all seemed to be cautionary tales—sad drones who were never getting out of here. But Emma still longed for a full-time position and the slight pay increase it would bring.

She carefully placed the next grotesque pumpkin on the shelf. Even without going full-time, she'd probably have enough money for a used car by next year, between SaveMart and her other source of income. Then she could leave, look for a better job somewhere else. Of course it would likely be an equally crummy job—twenty-year-olds with only a high school diploma didn't have many options—but a girl could dream.

Mollie, who was barely older than Emma but already a manager because she'd been to college, came over to check out her progress. "Looking good."

"It looks like something out of a horror movie," she said, because she could be honest with Mollie. "You know they're not going to sell, right?"

"Maybe someone will need haunted house décor. Or there'll be an ugly jack-o'-lantern contest. We'll unload some of them, anyway."

Emma shrugged. It wasn't her problem; best not to think about it.

"How's the ghostie business going? This must be your busy season," Mollie said, running her finger over a particularly misshapen pumpkin.

"Yeah, it's not bad."

"I'm having a party on Halloween, if you don't already have plans."

Emma paused. "You want me to . . ."

"No, no, not a séance. I wouldn't monkey with that stuff for the world. No offense. I just meant as a guest. As a friend."

"Oh," Emma said, embarrassed by the misunderstanding. She and Mollie got along fine, but they weren't that close. Were they? Emma had avoided work friendships after Finn, who thought they were more than friends and tried to kiss her in the break room. She'd pushed him away and they'd both stammered apologies—Emma wasn't sure what she'd said, hadn't listened to what Finn said, either—before never making eye contact again. Finn, a fellow part-timer, had quit the following month, and now worked at the pizzeria on the Boulevard, which Emma carefully avoided.

She realized Mollie was looking at her expectantly. "Um, maybe? If the party I'm working lets out early enough, I guess."

"Cool. Don't worry, it's not a work thing. Just friends from school and stuff. You'll fit right in."

Would she? Doubtful. She never seemed to fit in anywhere. "Right. Thanks for inviting me." She laughed nervously and reached for another pumpkin, feeling a sudden kinship to it. She was a SaveMart pumpkin, and everyone else was a normal one.

When she looked up again, Mollie was gone.

After work she unchained her bicycle from the rack and headed for a gig in the next town. Mollie had been correct; the ghostie business thrived in October. Tonight's séance was a small gathering of bored housewives, Emma's favorite kind of customers.

She'd discovered she'd had the talent last Halloween, during a party at her neighbor Cleo's house. They weren't that close, but Cleo had invited everyone who was still around from their high school class, and Emma couldn't think of a reason not to go. It had been stupid stuff mostly—drinking, video games, posing for pictures in the life-sized coffin Cleo's dad had built—but then Cleo's cousin Nyla had brought out a Ouija board and said she could conjure up dead loved ones. Had anyone believed her? Maybe not. They'd just been fooling around, feeling silly and more than a bit tipsy. As usual Emma was on the edge of things, debating whether she should just sneak home.

But Nyla insisted it was real, invoking the names of dead relatives in a way that cast a pall over the evening, particularly when the supposed ghost's messages were all generic and cliché. Nyla kept saying that hers should be the only finger on the planchette, which surely wasn't in the spirit of things. Yet no one protested or wandered off, as though the mere promise of something spectral and supernatural was a powerful adhesive. Their expectancy held them there even as Nyla disappointed them again and again.

Then, in the midst of an impeccably spelled but extremely boring message that was supposedly from Tina's grandmother, Emma became aware of an agitated woman standing behind Nyla. At first the woman's mouth moved silently, as though lip-synching a song only she could hear, but eventually Emma could make out what she was saying, first at a whisper and then at increasing volume, until she opened her own mouth and repeated the woman's words.

"That girl's all wrong, all wrong! I'm not saying that at all! Tina, love, you know I don't talk like that. You need to stop seeing that Danny. He's no good for you, love. Trust me, Gamma knows."

Of course everyone stared at Emma—Nyla with resentment, most everyone else with open-mouthed shock, Tina with tears running down her face. "Gam?" she said, voice breaking, and Emma found herself nodding even as she longed to run away and hide somewhere. What had she been thinking, making such a spectacle of herself?

Instead she said, "Love you, my little parsnip," because that's what Tina's grandmother was urging her to say, and this strange endearment caused Tina to laugh and sob at the same time. Tina's grandmother nodded at Emma like she'd done exactly right, and Nyla shoved the planchette across the Ouija board and said this was a stupid game and they should make margaritas, and most of the crowd seemed more than ready to agree.

When everyone had left the room except Tina and one other girl that Emma didn't know, Tina said, "Was that real?"

The grandmother was gone now, and Emma was tempted to say, "No" or "I don't know" or "I really hope not," but instead she said, "I think so" because she knew that was what Tina wanted to hear, and she also thought it was the truth, much as she didn't want it to be.

Tina thanked her, smiling through her tears, and drifted away, and the other girl said, "Could you do it again?"

"I don't . . ."

"Please?" she asked, her voice begging and desperate. "It's my brother, he died last year . . ."

"I'm sorry," Emma said, the automatic response to anyone's grief.

"Could you just . . . try? His name is Wyatt."

"Wyatt," Emma repeated, scanning the empty room, praying she wouldn't see anyone. But suddenly there he was, a skinny, hollow-eyed specter of a boy lurking behind his sister.

"Tell her it's all her fault," he moaned. "Tell her I'll never forgive her! Tell her!"

"He says it's not your fault," Emma said, looking deep into the girl's sad eyes while Wyatt raged behind her. "He wants you to forgive yourself, because he has."

The sadness in the girl's eyes overflowed into tears, and she squeezed Emma's hand and nodded and nodded, and Emma did her best to smile gently and ignore Wyatt howling in the background.

It might have been easy enough—well, perhaps not easy, but at least possible—to pretend the whole night never happened or had been some drunken hallucination, except no one else seemed willing to do that. People at that party kept bringing it up—laughingly if they were in a group, reverentially if they were alone with Emma. Was she for real? What, exactly, had happened? Would she be willing to do it again?

She wanted to deny it, wanted to say no, but whoever came asking—usually in the midst of a shift at SaveMart, which was doubly embarrassing—always looked so hopeful that Emma could never turn them down. After a while, she stopped wishing the ghosts wouldn't appear and just accepted that they would.

The ghosts never stayed long, which was a relief. She didn't think she could stand being haunted all day long. She tried not to think about the whys too much, but the ghosts only seemed to show up through the combined efforts of Emma's presence and the ardent wish of whoever wanted them summoned. They'd say their piece, Emma voicing their words with a varying degree of accuracy, depending on the message, and then they'd disappear. Simple enough, and not too nightmare inducing.

The business developed throughout the year. Word spread and people she didn't know started contacting her, weird chains of acquaintances' relatives' neighbors and so on. It was a middle-aged woman looking to speak to her recently deceased husband who first offered to pay her, and though Emma stammered out multiple refusals, the woman insisted she take the money. "You provide a vital service, honey. Don't undersell yourself."

She'd given Emma two hundred dollars like it was nothing, which felt exhilarating and dirty at the same time. A vital service. Well, why not? She made herself a Facebook page advertising what she could do and her fees. Over the next few months she honed the text and even created a name for this strange little side hustle: In the Spirit of Fun. It helped attract the right clientele: boozy women looking for party tricks rather than grieving spouses or, worse yet, parents.

She learned to say no if it wasn't the kind of séance she wanted to do. No children's parties (yes, two separate mothers had asked). No child ghosts. No men who asked her to send a picture of herself before they'd book her. A gentle but firm no to anyone who sounded too sad, too desperate.

Tonight's séance went fine. After reminding the women that she couldn't summon dead celebrities—she'd tried many times with no success, and finally settled on the line, "It has to be someone you know personally," because that was more tactful than, "No one famous wants to talk to you"—it had been mostly grandparents. Those were the best kind of ghosts, in Emma's opinion: some gentle *I love you's* and *I miss you's*, some sweet recollections, nothing overwrought. They lacked all the complications of parents or lovers.

The perfect relationship. Emma wondered if she could skip over all of life's landmines and just become a grandparent.

The only unnerving thing was the girl. She'd popped up at the last three séances Emma had held, the only ghost she'd ever seen more than once. She was strangely solid, too, so much so that Emma had thought she'd been a party guest the first time, had nearly asked her who she wanted to contact before realizing her mistake. The girl didn't speak the whole night; apparently none of the guests had summoned her, and she hadn't clamored to speak to any of them. A bit strange, but Emma didn't give it much thought.

When the girl appeared at the next séance, though, Emma noticed. It was two towns over from the last one, with none of the same guests. What was this girl—this ghost—doing there? She couldn't very well ask, not in the midst of a crowd. Once again the ghost girl didn't talk, and no one asked to talk to her.

This time Emma kept a closer eye on her. Not a very old ghost, either in age or time dead, as her clothes—a band T-shirt for First Aid Kit, a flannel shirt, and leggings—didn't look out of place. She had black eyeliner that was on point, dark hair in a single braid, and side-swept bangs. At the end of the night she disappeared with the rest of the ghosts, and yet Emma still felt uneasy, like the ghost girl was lurking just out of sight. And now here she was again, for a third time.

She waited until that night, alone in her bedroom, to call the ghost back again. She'd never tried to summon a ghost on her own before; mostly because there were none she really wanted to see, but also because it seemed like it should be a multi-person thing, a spectacle. She half-hoped she wouldn't be able to do it solo, but she'd no sooner thought about the ghost girl than she materialized in the room, smiling as though she was happy to be invited.

"What's your name?" Emma asked, keeping her voice low even though she knew her father was a heavy sleeper.

"Steffi," the girl said. She looked around Emma's age or a little younger, bouncing on the balls of her feet like this was an important interview she didn't want to mess up.

"I'm Emma."

"I know!"

Emma ignored that and got to the point. "Why have you been hanging around my séances?"

Steffi's smile dimmed a bit. "They're kind of interesting."

So Steffi was . . . bored? That was how poltergeists started, wasn't it? No, she couldn't think like that; this wasn't a horror movie. "Did you know anyone at the séances?"

Steffi shook her head.

"It's just that normally someone has to want to see you. For you to appear, I mean."

Steffi was silent for a moment. "That's how it works?" she asked finally.

Emma wanted to say she didn't know, that no one had given her an instruction manual for ghosts, but instead she just said, "Usually."

"Huh."

"So do you have someone you want to talk to? Maybe that's why you're here? You have some, I dunno, unfinished business I could help you with?"

"Meaning if I finish my business, I'll disappear?" Steffi asked guardedly.

It would be nice, but probably not what she wanted to hear. "Have you been dead long?" Emma asked gently.

"Since 2011."

"Thirteen years," Emma said, watching Steffi's face carefully. Did she know she'd been a ghost that long? Her expression didn't change, so Emma asked, "Have you been . . . hanging around all this time?"

Steffi shrugged like she didn't want to talk about it, but then said, "It's nice to finally have someone to talk to."

Oh, God. She had not signed up for this.

Emma tried again. "Is there someone I can help you talk to? Your parents? Siblings?" It dawned on her that reverse engineering a séance—finding the living people instead of the ghosts—would be awkward at best and difficult at worst, but it was still better than being haunted by a stranger, wasn't it?

Steffi frowned slightly. "I had three older siblings, but I wasn't close to any of them. My mom was forty-six when she had me.

Definitely an accident. My siblings were already teenagers, and they all left home by the time I started kindergarten. My parents were nice people, but they were kind of done with kids by then. We weren't really close."

Emma considered suggesting that perhaps Steffi was wrong, that of course her parents would want to hear from her, but in truth she understood. She hadn't heard from her own mother in years, and she and her father existed more as roommates than family. If she died tomorrow, would he even miss her, other than the money she contributed to the household bills? Probably not. No use lying to herself.

She tried again. "A boyfriend, then? Or a girlfriend?"

"Why doesn't anyone ever ask about friend-friends?"

Because they'd been programmed by society to believe that romantic love mattered more than anything else? She didn't say that though, just asked, "A friend-friend, then?"

Steffi flicked the question away with the wave of a hand. "Nah. There's no one." She paused. "Maybe my unfinished business is something else. Do you have *The Big Black and the Blue*?"

"What?"

"It's an album. By First Aid Kit. Maybe I need to hear it one more time before I can move on."

Emma rolled her eyes, but pulled Spotify up on her laptop anyway. She nearly handed Steffi her headphones before realizing that would be stupid.

So they listened together. It wasn't terrible, even with Steffi singing along to every track. Emma almost told her to keep it down, then remembered no one else could hear her.

They listened to the entire album, and Steffi was still there. "Thanks for trying," she said.

"Uh, you're welcome. I'm going to get ready for bed now," she said, heading for the bathroom and praying that Steffi wouldn't be there when she came back.

She wasn't, but somehow it wasn't the relief Emma had thought it would be.

Steffi turned up again at the next séance three days later, giving Emma a tiny wave and a smile and not looking offended when Emma didn't acknowledge her. One of the ghosts that night was the worst kind—hysterical and shrieking, not giving Emma anything to work with. She made up her own answers to the client's queries, though the more upset the ghost grew, the harder it was to concentrate or to hear what the client was saying.

"You need to calm down," Steffi finally said to the ghost, sounding impressively commanding. "I know she's being frustrating, not getting your message across . . ." she shot Emma a faintly accusatory look, "but it's hard to listen to you when you're caterwauling like that. It's understandable that you're excited, but maybe take a minute to collect yourself and try again."

Much to Emma's surprise, the ghost took Steffi's advice. After ten seconds of silence, he started speaking again, quickly but more understandably, a long and only slightly convoluted story about why the client shouldn't trust her uncle. Not the kind of drama Emma usually liked to involve herself with, but Steffi motioned for her to go on so she did, relaying everything, more or less word for word. The client seemed grateful afterwards, and even gave her a twenty dollar tip.

She didn't see Steffi again until after she'd left. The ghost stood by her bicycle, looking even more solid than usual. "You shouldn't mess with people's words like that."

Emma shrugged. "Sometimes it's just easier."

"That doesn't make it right."

"Are you haunting me just to lecture me?"

Steffi sighed. "You're the only one who can see me. Besides, we have a connection."

"A connection?" Did Steffi think they were friends? Or did she know something Emma didn't, like they were actually second cousins or something?

"That's my bike."

"Seriously?" She'd gotten the bike at a yard sale after she started the séance thing and needed a way to get around more. It was hard to find cheap adult bicycles and price had been her only criteria, yet she'd wound up with the perfect bike for her business: black with silver stars stenciled on the frame and silver tassels streaming from the handlebars. Effortlessly quirky, with a touch of witchiness.

"Mm-hmm," Steffi said. "Used to be mine. Why do you do it, though? The séances."

"Because I can." An inadequate response; she knew that even before the words left her mouth. Just because you could do something didn't mean you *should*. "It makes me feel special," she said more quietly. "Like I'm not a twenty-year-old loser living in her father's house, not going to college, with a sad little job in a sad little town. Even when I feel uncomfortable doing it, I know it's the only interesting thing about me. I *hate* that it's the only interesting thing about me."

She couldn't believe she'd said all that, but Steffi was nodding hard. Not in a *Yes, I agree you're dull* way, but in an *I understand completely* way. It felt warm, that nod.

"Sometimes I feel like such a freak," Emma added. Not sometimes. Most of the time. All of the time. "Better to be the freak that sees ghosts. At least other people seem to enjoy that. And it's lucrative."

"What are you using the money for?"

It was turning into Twenty Questions, but Steffi's frankness was kind of refreshing. "I'm saving up for a car."

Steffi looked aghast. "What do you want a car for?"

Was she kidding? "Um, let's see. Ease of transport. I can go further. Be warmer. Get away from this place."

"Bikes are better. Especially this one."

"It's a lovely bike," Emma conceded. "But realistically I can't ride more than twenty miles or so out of town, and it's no fun in winter."

Steffi kept talking like she hadn't heard her. "It used to be my older sister's. I feel like everything I ever owned used to be somebody else's first. But I'm the one who painted it black and put the stars and streamers on. It really felt like mine then. I used to ride all the way out to Ashford Park—you know where that is?"

Emma nodded. It was a good ten miles away.

"I'd go out there on a Saturday evening and ride the bike paths. It was always pretty empty because people thought they had better things to do, but there was really nothing better than that. Zooming along on my bike, feeling like I was the last person on Earth. You should try it sometime."

Emma made a noncommittal noise, but it did sound kind of nice.

She thought she'd left Steffi at the séance, but once she got home, the ghost showed up again. Emma put *The Big Black and the Blue* on again, and it wasn't such a bad evening.

Steffi appeared most nights after that. At the séance, if Emma had one, but then after in her room, too. Did she come because Emma had started to expect her and therefore had her on her mind, or was it out of Emma's control? She wasn't sure.

When Emma got sick of listening to *The Big Black and the Blue*, she finally told Steffi that First Aid Kit had, in fact, released other albums in the past thirteen years, and they listened to all of those so many times that the songs were constantly stuck in Emma's head, a soundtrack to her mundane days that she found she didn't mind. One time at SaveMart she hummed "My Silver Lining" without even realizing it until Mollie started singing along. "I love that song!"

"Me, too," Emma said. When she told Steffi about it that night, the ghost said, "I've converted you!" and laughed so joyfully that Emma joined in.

They watched stuff together, too, *The Office* or *Taskmaster*, because Emma needed something light and silly, especially after a séance. Maybe Steffi did, too.

Steffi was always gone come morning. Was she lurking somewhere, invisible, or did she flit back-and-forth between here and some unknowable afterlife? Emma didn't ask, didn't really want to know. Talking to ghosts was bad enough; there would be no coming back from finding out all the intricacies of death.

They did talk about some things, though. Steffi confessed that she'd felt invisible even when she was alive. "My family never really listened to me. They wanted me to fit into some cute kid sister box, and they ignored the fact that I grew out of it ages ago."

"Everyone always wants people to fit in a box," Emma agreed.

"Especially when you're dead," Steffi said pointedly. "I can't even be the right kind of ghost and find my peace and disappear for you."

Emma wanted to say she didn't want Steffi to disappear, but instead she said, "Maybe I'm just the wrong kind of medium."

When Steffi didn't say anything, she went on. "I know about boxes. People expecting you to be one thing or another. Expecting you to . . ." She swallowed, trying to find these words she'd never dared say to anyone before. Did a ghost count as an anyone?

"Expecting you to what?" Steffi asked.

Of course Steffi was someone. "To want to be with someone. In a . . . you know . . . intimate way." The words sounded cringey even to her. She wanted to disappear. She wanted to—

"You're asexual!" Steffi said, sounding so delighted that Emma giggled even as she felt her cheeks flame even hotter.

"I didn't know you knew about that," she mumbled.

Steffi sucked her teeth. "I've been dead thirteen years, not thirty!"

"We say ace now," Emma said, as though she was actually part of a community. As though she'd identified herself as such to anyone other than Steffi.

"Ace," repeated Steffi with a certain reverence. "What?" she added, and Emma realized she'd been staring.

"You're just so . . . accepting."

Steffi frowned, "Why wouldn't I be?"

"You'd be surprised how many people insist it isn't a thing. Or that you'll change your mind. That there's something wrong with you. That you just haven't met the right person yet." She didn't add that the main voice saying these things was her own, a constant refrain in her head.

"I'm not surprised, actually," Steffi said. "I'm not surprised at all."

Emma looked her in the eyes. Steffi looked back. So many things could be said with a look.

"Can we change the subject?" Emma asked, averting her gaze.

"Um . . . do you enjoy the séances?"

"They're sad, mostly."

"Do I make you sad?"

"No," she said quickly. *You make me the opposite of sad.* She'd said so much tonight, but somehow she couldn't bring herself to say that.

The next night was Halloween, and she'd been hired for a party at a big house in Greenwood. She wheeled her bike up the path past a row of perfectly round pumpkins that clearly had not come from SaveMart. Inside, the hostess, Ana, introduced Emma to the guests and motioned to a punch bowl of green, noxious-looking liquid. "Would you like some witch's brew?"

It was definitely alcoholic and looked truly disgusting, with a scummy film punctuated with candy eyeballs. "I see the ghosts better when I'm sober," she said, which wasn't entirely true, but was always a wise route to take. She made better decisions about which messages to pass on and which to edit when sober, anyhow, and got less emotional. Once after two shots of sambuca, she'd embarrassed herself by sobbing over the hostess's dead boyfriend's message, to the point that the ghost had left in disgust.

"A cupcake, then?" Ana pressed one into her hand without waiting for a reply, neon orange frosting with a chocolate spider on top. "Your fortune's inside."

"Hmm?"

"Bite in, you'll see."

It took two bites to get to the middle of the cupcake, where her teeth hit a small plastic baggy. Emma tugged it out and opened it to reveal a gaudy-looking ring.

"That means you're getting married soon!" Ana said, clapping her hands like an excited little girl.

"Thanks," Emma mumbled, putting down the cupcake and slipping the silly ring into her pocket.

Eventually, everyone was led to an impressively large table with a lacy black cloth, and Emma summoned the ghosts. A whole slew of them: grandparents, a poignant father, a tragic ex. She passed on everyone's messages accurately, though she couldn't resist throwing in some dramatic pauses. She wished Steffi was there to see her masterful performance. Where was she tonight? She was always at Emma's séances.

Afterwards, everyone wanted to talk to her, but she made excuses. She kind of wanted to give Mollie's party a try, maybe pretend she had a real flesh-and-blood friend for a night. She exited the house, only to be halted by a voice behind her.

"Are you for real?"

She turned to see one of the guests, a frowning thirty-ish woman with tired eyes and a kitty-ear headband. Emma was pretty sure her name was Caitlin.

"As real as you want me to be." It was an answer she'd practiced, trying to find just the right balance between flippancy and sincerity in both her tone and the accompanying smile.

"Could—would you—that is, I've got someone I'd like to speak to. Not in front of everyone else. Could we do it out here?"

"Who is it?" Emma asked carefully.

"A friend. Or she was. She might not be so friendly anymore, considering I killed her."

Emma took an involuntary step back, frantically adding 'no murderers' to her mental list of refusals.

"Not like that," Caitlin said quickly. "I didn't, like, plunge a knife into her chest or anything. I just . . . feel responsible." She shook her head. "It's my fault she died."

"I'm sorry for your loss." Another practiced line, though tonight her voice shook slightly.

"I thought maybe if I tried to apologize . . ."

She didn't finish, and Emma wasn't sure what was meant to fill the empty silence. Did she think apologizing would make her feel better? Surely that wasn't how guilt worked.

"What's her name?"

"Steffi."

Two syllables jolting against her chest. Of course she must mean someone else. Surely there were other dead Steffis.

Did she like First Aid Kit? Have nice bangs? Own a black bike with stars on it? She didn't ask any of these questions because she was too scared of the answers.

"Think about her and she might come," she said instead. Caitlin nodded and closed her eyes, screwed up her face, as though remembering took an enormous amount of mental energy. Emma waited for a spirit to appear, willing it to be a stranger, some different Steffi she'd help Caitlin make her peace with.

No one came.

Emma found herself squinting, as though this might somehow help. In the dim glow of the porch light, she could see Caitlin's face growing pink, like she might strain something.

"Is she . . ." Caitlin whispered.

"I . . ." There was still no one there, but Caitlin looked so hopeful. "I'm getting someone, faintly. Does Steffi have dark hair?"

"Yes."

"Perfect eyeliner? A First Aid Kit shirt?" *Please say no.*

"Oh my God! Yes, that's her!" Caitlin's eyes sprang open, her gaze darting around wildly as if she might be able to see Steffi, too.

"Like I said, she's very faint," Emma said. She felt like she was talking under water, the words distorted and hard to enunciate. She wanted to run away, hop on her bike, pedal until she was somewhere far from here. She wanted to be alone, except when she pictured alone, Steffi was there, too.

But she wasn't alone, and she wasn't with Steffi. All she had was this devastated woman who wanted her help.

She led Caitlin further down the long porch, further into the shadows. Caitlin was trembling, and Emma's own knees felt strangely weak. "Say what you want her to hear," she told Caitlin.

Caitlin nodded, but didn't say anything at first. She shut her eyes again, swaying slightly. "Steffi?" Her voice sounded younger, on the verge of tears. "I think about you all the time. All the stuff we used to do together. You remember those knock-off My Little Ponies we had in second grade? They were your sister's, all smudgy and gross, but we thought they were the best thing ever. We made up so many stories about them, remember? And middle school glee club, when you used to imitate Mrs. Mortimer behind her back, and that one time she turned around and . . ."

Caitlin was crying outright now, and Emma felt like crying, too. She still couldn't see Steffi-the-ghost, but glimpses of second grade Steffi and middle school Steffi flitted around her peripheral vision.

"I never meant to hurt you. I love you, Steff, you know that. You were my best friend, and I never meant to . . . freak you out. Make you feel like you had to run away from me. I'm so sorry. Please tell me you know how sorry I am."

"She knows," Emma said, gently squeezing Caitlin's hand. The words came from some automatic place that she drew on during every séance; she knew she shouldn't say them, but she couldn't seem to help herself. "She doesn't want you to feel bad. She loves you, too."

Caitlin sobbed, scrubbed a hand over her face, and then looked at Emma. "How do I know she's really saying that? I thought I could believe, but . . . I can't . . . I don't . . ."

Emma didn't know what to say, what to do. Should she apologize? Confess that Steffi wasn't actually here? Put an arm around Caitlin's shoulder and hold her while she cried? Go find someone inside, a real adult who would surely comfort Caitlin better than she could? She never knew what to do, never . . .

"Tell her to stop being a self-pitying baby. Tell her I still think Peach Jubilee is the stupidest pony name on earth, and she needs to get over herself. Tell her it's time to move on."

Steffi, eyes blazing, appeared behind Caitlin, spitting out the words like a hail of bullets. Emma couldn't tell if the fury was directed at her or Caitlin. Possibly both of them. Emma didn't know what Caitlin had done, but she knew how Steffi felt when she put words in ghosts' mouths.

She repeated Steffi's words verbatim. How could she not? She watched as Caitlin's eyes filled with wonder, a small smile breaking through the tears. "Now that sounds like Steffi. She's really here?"

"Yes," Emma said simply, daring to glance at the still furious Steffi.

"I'm sorry, Steff," Caitlin said, voice trembling. "So, so sorry. I love you."

"Tell her . . ." Steffi's voice was choked with something, and Emma felt the urge to clear her own throat. "Tell her I love her, too.

And then tell her I'm gone. Disappeared." When Emma just stared at her, she added, "What? It's only okay to lie when you come up with it yourself? *Tell her*!"

So Emma did.

Caitlin took a shaky breath, the tears still streaming down her face. "Thank you. I never thought . . . it's been so awful . . . how she . . . how I . . ."

"Make her shut up," Steffi moaned.

"Shhh, shh," Emma soothed, putting an arm around Caitlin and moving her back toward the front door. "It's all right now. You heard her. She wants you to move on. She loves you."

She delivered Caitlin to Ana, stumbling through some sort of excuse that probably didn't make much sense. She didn't care. She had to get back outside, back to Steffi. What if she wasn't there?

But she was. "You had no right!" Steffi said, her voice low and terrible. "Putting words in my mouth like that."

"I'm sorry," she said quickly.

Steffi shook her head. "I hate how you do that. Make up what you think we should say. Like we don't matter. Like you know best. Like the living and their need to feel better matter more than the dead."

Emma opened her mouth to try to protest, to justify it, but then she closed it again, unable to think of anything to say. Of course she shouldn't have done what she'd done. Of course it was inexcusable.

Steffi darted off the porch and paced up and down the path, her feet blurring through the pumpkins. Emma followed, afraid Steffi might disappear, disintegrate, go wherever it was she went that Emma had always been too scared to ask about.

"I thought we were friends," Steffi said. "But a friend doesn't do stuff like this."

The words burned in her ears. "I know. I'm sorry. She just seemed so . . . sad." She knew it was a stupid excuse even before Steffi huffed her disapproval. "I don't like it when people are upset," she said, trying to explain. "But now I've made you upset, and that's even worse."

She watched Steffi pace up and down, up and down, and wished she could take her hand. "Do you want to talk about it?" she asked quietly. "What happened with Caitlin?"

Steffi scowled. "Oh, you're dying to know what happened, aren't you? Why don't you ask her?"

Because I don't want you to disappear. Because if I keep you talking, maybe you can find it in yourself to forgive me.

"Because you're the one who's my friend," she said.

Steffi continued pacing. "Caitlin and I were best friends," she said finally. "Just like she said. Ponies with dumb names when we were kids. Secret handshakes and dance moves. We just got each other, you know? Or at least I thought we did."

"What happened?"

"After graduation, I tried to . . . come out to her. Tell her I was . . . ace. I should have done it ages ago, when she told me she was gay, but I didn't have it all figured out then, didn't know how to . . ."

Emma nodded. The very idea of telling anyone other than Steffi about her sexuality made her break out in a cold sweat.

"But I thought I was finally ready. We were in her car, parked down by the canal after work because neither of us wanted to go home. I did a shit job of telling her. I said something about being different like her, about not having feelings for boys . . . I couldn't get out the part about not having feelings for girls, either. It was terrible, and the more flustered I got, the more Caitlin seemed to get the wrong idea, and then she took my hand and said she always knew I was gay, and I just . . . I just . . ."

Emma shuddered, imagining herself in Steffi's place. How terrible it would be to have the person who knew you best misunderstand you like that.

"I freaked out," Steffi said. "She looked so pleased, like she had me all figured out, put me into another box, and—I mean, it was just so stupid, of course I could have explained, and she would have been fine with it, but . . . instead I just bolted. Got out of the car and took off in a blind panic. Ran into the street and got hit by a semi thirty yards from the canal."

For a moment Emma saw it play out, could feel the impact of a twenty-ton truck crushing her ribs. "That's terrible," she gasped.

"I know. And of course it wasn't Caitlin's fault. She shouldn't have spent the last thirteen years of her life feeling guilty. I don't blame her. But that doesn't mean I want you giving her absolution on my behalf, either."

"I'm sorry," Emma repeated. She took a deep breath. "Sometimes I think I do it because séances are the only time people actually listen to me. The only time I ever have anything important to say. So I try to make sure it's what they want to hear."

"By making things up?" The anger was back in Steffi's voice. "And what do you mean no one ever listens to you outside of séances? I listen to you. Don't I count?"

"Of course you count," Emma said quickly.

Steffi finally stopped pacing. She was still frowning, but she looked straight at Emma. "Then tell me something. Tell me something important, something you want to say, not something you think I want to hear."

For a moment she froze, afraid of saying the wrong thing, but then the words came pouring out. Her words. "You're the best friend I've ever had. The only person I can talk to. The only person who accepts me for the misshapen SaveMart pumpkin that I am." Oh God, she was babbling. She took a deep breath and plowed on. "I love you, in a completely platonic way that I've never felt before. And I'm terrified that you hate me now. Or that you'll disappear and I'll never see you again."

The moment seemed to stretch for eons. Emma found she couldn't look at Steffi, could only stare at the perfect pumpkins. She had the urge to smash one, but she didn't think it would make her feel any better.

"Where would I go?" Steffi finally asked.

"Wherever you disappear to when you're not here. I've always been too scared to ask about where that is."

"I don't know," Steffi said quietly. "I can never remember, once I'm here. Maybe it's just nothingness."

Emma shuddered.

"But I always come back, don't I? I wasn't sure why at first, but now I think I know. You draw me here. Like I'm meant to be with you."

Emma could feel her heart pounding in her chest, like every corny romance story she'd ever read but never believed. "So you don't hate me?"

"I am still mad at you," Steffi said, though before Emma's heart completely stopped, she added, "but I love you, too."

Emma laughed. It bubbled out of her, a release, a relief, a realization. This was what it felt like to be worthy of someone's love, to be loved in the way she actually wanted to be loved.

"Should we go home and watch *Taskmaster*?" Emma asked, before her emotions completely overwhelmed her.

"I thought you were going to Mollie's party?"

"I'd rather be with you."

"Nah, you should go. *Taskmaster* can wait until later." When Emma gave her a skeptical look, she added, "You need some living friends, too."

Emma retrieved her beautiful bike that had once been Steffi's. "Keep me company on the ride over?"

Steffi grinned, "Sure."

Emma started pedaling, picking up speed as she went, feeling like she was the last person on Earth, except she wasn't, because Steffi was behind her, singing "My Silver Lining" at the top of her lungs. The night was awash with possibilities and friendship, and she never wanted it to end.

Clocks

N. Anaar

Estella's father's study was exactly as he left it.

His jacket hung on his tall chair—never on the coat hanger, but never crumpled either. The inkwell on the oak desk was just above half full. Perhaps the stack of papers was a bit too large—but always in a neat pile.

And, of course, the clocks.

They were all over the workspace, even the finished ones. But Estella understood that her father planted his chaos *deliberately*. The small clocks placed in front of the larger ones; the gear train always accessible; the Samhain clock always at the very back—to be spoken to again.

She had no memory of her mother; until she met Angie, her father had been her entire world. They had eaten together, cleaned together, danced together—and on her twelfth birthday, they had spoken a clock together. He had never sold it. But the past few months it had been too painful to see hanging on the wall each day. She had given it to Angie, who had faithfully hidden it.

If he resented sharing her with Angie, he never showed it. Angie was good at speaking. Estella supposed he would have accepted a tortoise, so long as they were dedicated to speaking. But, how much did Estella truly want Angie to do around the workshop?

The in-progress clocks were still and silent. Almost watching her. *When it chimes for the first time, you'll know it's done being spoken to.*

She looked at last year's Samhain clock. She only had a few more hours. Once it was dark out it would be time to move on. She'd been smart enough to not promise this year's clock to anyone. Angie hadn't agreed. *There's no reason you can't do this. I can help you.*

Maybe Angie thought it was grief that kept her from accepting the offer. Grief. A moment alone with her father's clocks. She'd told Angie they would meet at Angie's parents later. They would drink cider and eat pie and *move on*.

Estella herself had made some beautiful ones. A robin's egg blue one the size of a teacup—she'd told the gear a story about a bird's nest outside; how the chicks all found the right time and flew away. A green and purple springtime clock—she had described the time when the first flowers bloomed. Her father had displayed her "Whimsical Clocks" in the window. Eye-catching.

Girls' clocks. Cute. Silly. Nothing like the regal Samhain clock he oiled every year—taller than she was, with four golden turrets, one in each corner on the very top—that he kept in the back. Clients from all over the world came to view his regal clock. But he'd wanted *her* to inherit it.

She realized she was crying when a tear hit the mahogany dial. Her father had never indicated he wanted a son. He sent his daughter to school and taught her clock making. *At least she'd find a good husband to care for the business; make proper clocks and not some trinkets.* Had he thought that? His own father certainly would have. She'd brought home Angie. He welcomed her with a hug and a meal.

She caressed the clock face. *I will be worthy of your faith in me.*

All clocks must be spoken to once. A Samhain clock hears its story *twice*.

Estella knelt. She pressed her forehead against the centerpiece. It was warm to the touch—alive. Waiting. Most clocks hear one version of their story, and then hum to life—chiming and ticking. Beautiful in whatever highbrow dining room or cozy living room they end up in. But Samhain clocks . . . somehow they are deeper.

"I give you this story of time. This story comes from the first Samhain. Every year—" No. Not right.

"I give you this story of time. This story comes from the first Samhain. In time you come to life; you will give this story back to me. Each Samhain our father Maehla blesses us. He who blessed the first clock, so his son may—"

Her voice cracked on a sob.

Had her father spoken these words to the clock, with a pregnant wife, dreaming of the son who would make mahogany clocks with him? Had he said this to the clocks, while his wife was dead and his daughter was asleep and no son was in his future? Had he said this to the clocks, thinking of his own father, his grandfather, the line of patriarchs that had passed down clocks?

He'd said this to the clocks while she held him, through coughs that timed themselves between sentences. He'd said this to the clock in front of her, then told her how much he loved her. This last clock they had assembled together—though in practice, she had done most of it. He was far too frail.

Maybe Angie thought it was grief that kept Estella from accepting Angie's help. Maybe it was. Maybe it was resentment. Maybe Estella would never know.

She wrapped her arms around the clock. To her surprise, she could lift it easily. She tiptoed through the study, then slammed the door as she threw the clock at the banister.

"I give you this story of TIME!"

"I give you MY story of TIME!"

"It's time . . . ."

"Every Samhain . . . My father . . ."

Crying, she watched the clock fall. She meant to call for Angie, but it came out as a whisper.

It hit the ground. The wood flew up; the metal flew out. Dark brown pieces . . . and then they all just lay there.

Estella couldn't remember lying down, but at some point she woke up. The evening had changed from a light dusk to a dark one. Angie would be waiting, but she'd have to sweep up the clock first. She could never throw it away.

The past was the past. She needed to look forward. When tears burned again, she squeezed her eyes shut and kept them inside. She'd had a moment of weakness—nothing more. Next year's Samhain clock would be *ethereal*. She'd tell the town she was keeping this year's clock as a tribute. Nobody would judge her for that. If a broken clock stayed for years in the attic, until someday her own children found it—well, that was one thing. If she cried over the broken clock while her family got ready for dinner and dressed up for the town—well, whose business was that?

At the foot of the stairs she saw familiar mahogany wood. Familiar gears—she recognized the type of shining silver her father liked to speak to.

The crown of the clock wasn't at the top anymore—it was on the ground. And there were *two* crowns. Her father's mahogany, and a deep cherry red in the back. The gears in both were identical—and connected by a thick golden cord.

At the top was a seat. Under the seat, just off to each side, were two golden pedals. And right in front—the silver of the clock had turned into a shining handlebar. And, at the bottom, there was something entirely new. A pair of wheels, like on a cart or chariot. But instead of three or four, just two, of the exact same size.

She had never seen anything like it. She stroked the seat—it was soft, and warm to the touch. She would get to Angie's quickly, with this.

"It's time . . ."

Maybe it was her father's voice. Or maybe it was their voices blended—speaking together for the last time.

"Your time to go where you're going."

BOMBSHELL RED

JESSIE KWAK

Little things had made her start to wonder.

The way Justin knew the matches for the fireplace were hidden in the ceramic Oktoberfest beer stein on the mantle. The way he automatically twisted the shower knob right instead of left for hot water. The way he reached for the salt—in its little brown bear shaker on top of the microwave—without looking.

"We've been here Before, haven't we?" Sara asks.

"Of course not." That sharp, frustrated little breath is almost imperceptible, *almost*; Sara instantly regrets asking. But when Jason turns to her, it's with a weary smile. "I would tell you if you've been here Before."

Before, always with a capital B.

Because there are still so many places, so many details locked away in Sara's fuzzy memories from Before the car crash. Most of the time she can count on her vague sense of déjà vu and Justin's patience to slowly unearth those memories—especially in places she used to know and love.

But this cabin at the edge of the lake, with its wide porch covered in a sprinkling of dry pine needles, remains unfamiliar. The glittery neon pink beach cruisers leaning against the ping-pong table in the garage, the moose-themed quilt on the master bed, the novelty National Park drinking glasses—something should be pinging at her if they'd been here Before.

She would at least remember the unusual smell of the forest: sharp and piney and dry even in October, instead of the lush, ferny, rain-rich scent of the woods she grew up hiking in.

If she'd been here Before, she'd have had flashes of déjà vu by now.

And Justin would have told her.

Instead, he'd told her that a coworker had offered them this cabin. He'd said it would be nice to be out of town and away from the chaos of trick-or-treaters on their street for Halloween. Sara hadn't argued. She normally enjoys handing out candy, but Justin is probably right. This year, she's not certain she's up for it.

When they walk the trail to the lake overlook and Justin knows the right path without consulting the map, she almost asks him again—but she stops herself just in time. She doesn't need to keep accidentally reminding him of her crash. Reminding him that she's not yet whole, not while they're in this beautiful place, trying to relax. And so she trusts him, and tries to let herself enjoy a view without the disorienting, creeping dread that always waits on the edges of her consciousness.

At least Sara's stopped forgetting new *big* things, mostly, though when she's tired she drops pieces of conversation from earlier in the day, or misplaces items Justin swears he hasn't seen. And she *is* tired after the three-hour drive to the cabin, unpacking, and the hike out to the lake overlook. She'll shine it on for dinner—he made reservations at the boating club for their special Halloween night—but she's worn out. Which is probably why she can't find her mascara.

Because she just *had it*, didn't she? She absolutely did, the memory of seeing it in her toiletries bag is so strong, as is the weight of it in her fingers, the pleasure of setting it just so on the countertop and feeling pride in her improving dexterity—such a silly thing, but these days she'll take any win. She can picture it so clearly, and although she may not trust her mind fully anymore, there's no way she fabricated an entire memory from only moments ago, right?

She searches the counter another frustrating minute, digs through her jumbled bag of toiletries again, then finally spots it on the floor.

She did remember! Sara bends carefully to reach for it, still so uncertain of balance.

The tube rolls away before she can grasp it, must have been at the barest brush of her fingertips, she could have sworn she didn't touch it. It comes to rest beneath a cabinet.

The uneven floors on this old cabin, surely. Sara wedges her fingers beneath the cabinet and swears under her breath; her hand won't fit. She almost goes to ask Justin to help her move it—he'll chide her for trying to do it herself, if she aggravates her injury—but he was so relaxed when she left him out there on the porch. He deserves a moment of peace, after all this. And she used to be able to move much larger weights than this cabinet.

She sets her shoulder against it, finds purchase against the bathtub, and shoves.

The cabinet doesn't budge.

Sara tries again, giving a tiny grunt of pain as her still-healing shoulder twinges a complaint. Still nothing.

"Sara? Honey, do you need a hand?"

Justin's voice at the door sends Sara's pulse skyrocketing, and suddenly here's another memory let loose from the murky vault of Before: she's a senior in high school, about ten years earlier. It's a drizzly September day in Lebanon, Oregon, and she and her friend Sonya have snuck out under the bleachers at the football field to share a cigarette. They'd been leaning in close against the chill, Sonya's arm brushing Sara's, and—when Sara finished lighting the cigarette with clumsy fingers and looked up—her lips were so near Sara could have kissed her. Neither of them had moved at first, caught in the fragile moment. But then Sonya had shifted forward, ever so slightly. So had Sara.

And the janitor had turned the corner and yelled for them to get back to class.

Caught in the act—of smoking the cigarette, at least, the janitor hadn't seemed to notice the kiss. But neither girl ever went back under the bleachers.

Sara shakes off the powerful physicality of the memory, the girlhood fears of breaking rules that Justin sometimes dredges back up in her. If he opens the door now, he'll find her wedged between the cabinet and the bathtub, caught in the act of overexerting herself.

"All good," she calls back, getting to her feet too quickly. She can ask for his help getting the mascara later. They're in the middle of nowhere, after all. The boating club may recommend reservations, but Sara doesn't need to put on her full face.

Last month she might have felt more pressure to doll herself up, but now her competition is gone. The vows of marriage loyalty have won out. Justin chose her, in the end.

Not that he knows she knows.

"I'll just be a minute."

Sara finishes her eyeshadow and washes her hands, attention caught by the water swirling down the drain. Is it a trick of the light, or are the suds tinged pink? Bloody, almost as though she nicked a knuckle on the cabinet and didn't realize it; Sara studies her hands for a mystery cut, then freezes at the sudden chill touch at her neck.

Someone has swept back her hair. Cool lips brush her neck in a gentle kiss.

Justin, she thinks. Time must have skipped again and she didn't hear him open the door. But when she looks in the mirror it's not Justin she sees.

A trick of the eye. A trick of the light. A trick of her damaged, misfiring neurons—that's why there's another woman's face beside hers in the mirror. Bright red lipstick, thick lashes, flawless skin, honey-blond locks.

Sara blinks, expecting the image to clear, but the woman tilts her ruby red lips to Sara's ear. The lips form a single, malicious word, carried on a faint breath: *Run.*

Sara shrieks, shoving herself back from the sink and catching herself just before she would have stumbled over the toilet and crashed into the wall. She collapses on the lid of the toilet, heart pounding.

"Honey?"

Now Justin does burst in, brow pinched with worry, steady hands on Sara's shoulders. Warm and solid, not the ghostly-cool touch she'd imagined just a moment ago. She lets his touch ground her, lets that strong grip pull her back into reality as it has done again and again since her accident.

"I'm okay," she fibs. "I tripped on the rug."

"You need to be more careful," he tells her; it's his favorite phrase lately. He steadies her as she gets back to her feet, then kisses her brow. "Are you ready? You look beautiful."

She nods, still shaky, and turns to follow him out the door.

She risks a glance at the mirror, but sees only her mousy reflection.

Freia is gone.

She wasn't supposed to know about Freia, of course. One of this year's crop of interns at Justin's office, sweet and vibrant and game for adventure in ways that Sara hadn't been since Before.

When Sara had first found out—a text message from Freia on Justin's unlocked phone screen: *I miss you when can I see you again?*—she'd been livid. But she also needed to know more before she confronted him. By the time she'd learned enough to confirm she wasn't just making up the affair, he'd ended it. No more texts, no more emails, and she'd overheard Justin telling a coworker that Freia had left her internship early to move back to San Diego.

And through this whole time his patience with Sara had remained unwavering. He'd made a mistake, but he'd corrected it. He'd chosen Sara, in the end. She could be patient with him, too. This one time.

They're early for their reservation, so they park at the restaurant. They walk down to the lake's edge to watch water lapping at the pebbled beach, Justin holding Sara's arm as they navigate the unsteady terrain together. He kisses the top of her head as they watch the sun sink towards the rim of the mountains.

"It's so peaceful," she sighs. "Like it hasn't changed in thousands of years."

"It has changed, though," Justin says. "It used to be a river valley—remember, we drove by the dam?"

Sara doesn't remember a dam, but she nods like she does. "Of course. Right."

"The whole valley used to be filled with trees that were logged when the valley was flooded. Boaters have to be cautious of snags." He turns to her with a boyish smile that takes five years off his age, putting him closer to Sara's late twenties. "And the ghosts."

"Ghosts?"

The brush of lips on her neck, the chill of Freia's breath on her ear: RUN.

Sara shivers. Justin grins and slips his arm around her waist.

"The story goes that the local tribe used to fish at the rapids in the middle of the valley," he says. "Later, settlers built cabins all along the river bank. When they built the dam, all of that was drowned to create this reservoir."

"Did they give people time to move?"

"Of course. But they didn't move the graveyard. And one old settler refused to leave his farmstead. They say that if you're on the lake at night you can still see the glimmer of campfires and hearth fires far below, from ghosts whose graves were flooded. But you have to ignore them. Because if you stare, you'll attract the attention of the old man who drowned with his cabin, and he'll swim to the surface and reach his bony hand out to pull you down."

"Ridiculous," Sara says, with a smile to show she appreciates the story even though the thought makes her skin crawl. The peaceful surface of the lake could hide anything, she realizes. A glassy mirror reflecting clear blue sky while secrets swirl in its glacial currents.

The thought comes unbidden: *Old man or no, how many bodies are at the bottom of that lake?*

"Some say the campfires are just the reflection of the stars," Justin continues, still enjoying his tale. "They say it's an old superstition. Until that bony hand closes around their wrist."

His hand closes fast around hers, and Sara yelps, heart rate spiking.

Justin winks and lets her go, stepping away and pulling out his phone to frame up the golden path of evening light across the lake.

With the sun gone low, it's starting to get chilly. The wind soughs through the ponderosas behind them, like a voice calling *Sara, Sara, sarasarasara*. Sara stares down at the water lapping gently at her feet, and she can't help but think of drowned villages, generations upon generations of summer hunting camps wiped out, of the ghosts who must still return to dance on those drowned shores. How beautiful this place must be at night, though, the peaceful lake reflecting moon and stars, just as now it reflects the light of the dying sun.

At her feet the sun's last rays are caught in the ripples like flowing blond hair, twining in the current, parting around a bleached white stone like a skull.

The skull-like face in the water opens its eyes. Its bright red lips form a single word.

Run.

Sara screams, stumbling back from the edge of the lake. She catches herself on a boulder just before she goes down, her wrist wrenching painfully.

Justin is at her side in an instant. With the sun at his back his face is craggy and shadowed, eyes gleaming sharp with frustration or worry or something else, something darker and malicious. Sara's heart hammers in her chest, but it's just an illusion, there and gone so quick she can't possibly have seen it.

"What happened?" He sounds exasperated, patience with her wearing thin.

How can she explain it? *I thought I saw your lover, the one I'm not supposed to know about, drowned in the lake.* If she says she's seeing apparitions, their relaxing trip is over. Justin will insist on taking her home, putting her to bed, sending her back to the doctors. And she knows from experience that if she admits she knows about Freia, by the end of the conversation he'll have talked her in so many circles she'll believe she hallucinated the entire affair.

But most of all, if she believes she's seeing things, it will mean her months of progress have relapsed, that her unsteady mind and untrustworthy senses are disintegrating once more.

"It was a spider, I think," Sara says, and one of Justin's eyebrows goes skeptical. "It was on my shoe."

She tries for a sheepish grin. It works; Justin's smiling now, too, and he's shifted so the shadows around his eyes no longer seem menacing.

"Silly," he says, planting another kiss on her head, this one patronizing. She tries not to cringe, but she's the one who came up with such a ridiculous lie.

Either that or admit you're hallucinating and get sent back to the hospital.

"Where did you hear that story?" Sara asks as he helps her back to her feet. The sun has fallen behind the ridge, and now the surface of the lake is a strange matte gray, malleable and unsettling.

"What story?"

"About the ghosts in the lake?"

Justin blinks at her a second too long, then, "*Wikipedia*. I was doing some reading this afternoon while you were napping. I went down a rabbit hole."

"I thought you couldn't get service?"

Justin shrugs. "*You* can't, not with that ancient phone. Come on, we'll be late for dinner. And we'll talk about upgrading your phone when we get back home."

Sara smiles and accepts his arm to walk up to the restaurant, but the skin between her shoulder blades itches as she turns her back to the lake and its cold, deeply drowned secrets.

———·———

The unsettled déjà vu she'd felt back at the cabin returns with a vengeance as Justin walks past the restaurant's locked first door without even trying it, points out the specials sign Sara couldn't find, decides on Boneyard IPA without looking at the tap list, orders fried calamari before the waiter sets a menu down.

"Honey?"

She's studying the bait-and-tackle themed Halloween decor (a witch fishing for a skeletal fish, a pumpkin with a bass carved in the side) like something—anything—will jump out and tell her that she was here Before. The waiter has turned to her.

"I'm sorry," Sara says reflexively. She's not sure what she's apologizing for.

"Something to drink?" the waiter asks. "Chardonnay, right?"

"I don't drink," Sara says, and it's not until the waiter's startled look, his flash of a guilty glance at Justin, that the déjà vu snaps and the truth crystalizes.

She hasn't been here Before.

But Justin has.

With *her*.

"Sara? Honey, what's wrong?"

"I'm just feeling a little ill," she says, though ill hardly cuts it. She's reeling. It must have been the trip last month, which he'd told her was for a conference in Denver, though she hadn't been able to find his flight information. But she *had* found an unsubtle text from Freia with a bikini and sun emoji, and she'd assumed they'd gone to the coast for one last fling before Justin finally shut the affair down. But they'd come here, hadn't they?

"She drinks chardonnay, huh?" Sara asks before she can stop herself, and Justin's expression darkens.

"What are you talking about?"

"Freia." Sara doesn't care that the waiter is still standing at the table, that the couple in the booth across from them has started peeking looks. Something dark and furious flickers behind Justin's gaze, as fathomless and menacing as the lake with its drowned ghosts. "Cute, bubbly Freia." She pushes herself back from the table and to her feet, steadying herself against the usual wave of dizziness. "I need to go home."

For a moment she doesn't think Justin will follow, but, "I'm sorry about her," he says to the waiter before he stands himself. "Sara. Wait."

Sara didn't have a plan for getting back to the cabin. Even if she had the car keys she's still not cleared to drive, and she's not sure she'd remember the way. For a wild moment she thinks about heading off through the darkening woods, footsteps soft on a bed of dry pine needles. How long would she wander before she found their cabin? Or—and the thought thrills her—what if she never found it at all? She could be anyone she wanted, out there in the dark. Be *with* anyone she wanted.

But Justin catches her arm, steers her to the passenger seat, making the choice for her like he has so many times before.

The headlights flash on tree trunks as he drives, pale bones standing tall in the black forest. Justin's knuckles clenched on the steering wheel are white, too. "You made a scene back there," he says.

"More of a scene than you made when you came here with another woman?"

"That's not what we're talking about."

"So you admit it."

"Sara. Listen to yourself. Where are you *getting* this?"

"Your texts." Sara shifts in her seat to watch his face; he's glaring straight ahead. "Your emails."

"You're not even supposed to be looking at a computer with your concussion."

"You're not supposed to be sleeping around."

"And I wasn't." He swerves, a sudden, furious jerk around a pothole that Sara was unprepared for. Her shoulder thuds into the car door and panic spikes in her chest. The corner of Justin's mouth twitches; for a split second, it could have almost been a satisfied smile. "You're hallucinating."

"I know what I read."

"Can you even hear how crazy you sound, honey?"

"And I know it's over. That you called it off and she quit her internship and went back to San Diego." The headlights of a passing car blaze over Justin's face, but don't illuminate his eyes. When his face plunges back into darkness, they glint, as though a mask he's been wearing for the past few years has finally slipped off.

"You don't know what you're talking about," Justin says through clenched teeth.

Sara clutches the car door as he slams on the brakes in front of their cabin. Nausea swims through her gut, and she shoves the door open even as Justin shouts her name, ducking under the automatic garage door as it slowly grinds up. She pushes past the bicycles and the ping-pong table, her shaking hands rattling open the door to the house.

The nausea subsides by the time she makes it to the bathroom and slams the door behind her. She splashes water on her face, staring in the mirror. She almost expects the ghostly image of the other woman to appear again, but her own face is alone with its haggard, bloodshot eyes. Her cheeks are a blotchy red, but at least she doesn't have to worry about her mascara running, because she dropped it behind the—wait.

Is it her imagination, or has the cabinet been moved?

And the bathtub is full of water, now cool, though Sara doesn't remember drawing a bath. Had she done that before she left and forgotten? Had Justin?

She ignores the tub for now. The cabinet has definitely shifted, leaving a hand's width of space behind, and she *definitely* didn't do that. Her mascara is within reach—as is a tube of lipstick. Sara grabs them both, dropping the mascara back in her toiletries bag and studying the lipstick. It's called *Bombshell Red*. It looks just like the shade Freia wore.

But is that blood on the case?

Sara drops the lipstick tube in the sink, knees giving out. She would have fallen but for the arm around her waist, propping her up. She opens her eyes, startled, but it's not Justin. It's *her*, though Sara can't see her in the room, just in the mirror. Freia's blond hair is slicked back off her forehead, dripping like she's just gotten out of a shower or a bath. Her lips are tinged blue, her eyes bloodshot, her cheeks hollow. Her arm is a solid presence around Sara's waist, holding her close.

In the mirror, Freia strokes the back of her fingertips against Sara's cheek, and Sara shivers at the gentleness of the touch. Freia's hand traces down Sara's arm until her fingers twine through hers, then she picks up the lipstick and leans toward the mirror.

In the mirror, Sara can see Freia's hand guiding the lipstick. But when she looks away, she can only see the tube floating in midair. As though the mirror is finally showing her reality whereas her mind shows her only blank spaces where reality should be.

Sara turns back to the mirror and doesn't look away.

Freia is writing something with the lipstick, teeth caught on her full lip in concentration, and Sara is so taken by the charming nature of the gesture that she doesn't clock the words Freia is writing until Freia turns to her, handing her the lipstick tube and caressing Sara's cheek once more before vanishing. Sara turns back to find the blood red message on the mirror: *Run from him*.

"Sara."

Justin pushes open the bathroom door. His face is composed once more in concern, but Sara catches anger flickering beneath the cracks in the mask. He glances at the tub full of water, momentarily confused. "Are you going to take a bath?"

"What happened to her?"

"What are you talking about."

"To Freia." Sara's fist clenches around the lipstick tube. "What *happened* to her?"

I found out about you, I hadn't known he was married, the whisper twines through Sara's mind. *I was going to tell you everything. I was going to tell* everyone *everything.*

And then flashes of images: *The fight, the shove, the hastily drawn bath to finish the job, the blond hair drifting in the water, the midnight drive down to the lake with a sheet-wrapped burden weighed down with stones.*

"You killed her," Sara says. The way Justin's face hardens, she's never been more certain of anything in her life.

Still, she's not prepared when he lunges for her, grabbing her arm. His grip doesn't hold, though; his foot slips on the wet floor and he stumbles, splashing backwards into the bathtub. Sara could swear she hears a woman's laughter over his shout of fury.

Run.

She stumbles to the doorway, she means to follow Freia's warning and run, but she pauses in the doorway and sees that Justin hasn't pulled himself out of the tub. His feet kick, his hands clutching his own throat as he struggles. Sara can't see anything holding him down, but a face is reflected in the water, superimposed over his own staring eyes and gasping mouth. Blond hair, blood red lips.

Sara runs.

Ghostly laughter follows her as she dashes into the garage. Justin still must have the car keys in his pocket; even if she trusted herself to drive, she's not going back for them. The glittering pink beach cruisers gleam in the moonlight.

Sara grabs one, disentangling handlebars and pedals with a clatter. The second bike shifts where it's leaning, and for a moment Sara thinks it's going to fall. But then it rights itself and, wobbling at first, it begins to pedal itself out of the garage.

Sara doesn't stop to wonder why. She jumps on the other one and, after a few wobbles herself, begins to soar down the road, away from the cabin, towards her future.

When she risks a glance to her side, she catches blond hair streaming in the moonlight; when she holds out her hand, fingers entwine with hers. The bike ghosts along beside her. Sara rides.

Rebel Dispatch

Mildred Locke

Pedaling the unlit streets of Portland, you can't see the scars, the missing fingernails, or the gray tinge to my skin. I should break a sweat, pushing through into the Central Eastside Industrial District, rounding the corner and left onto Washington, but that would require a functioning central nervous system. Instead I pop a skid for fun, this deserted part of the city my playground.

I pass where the old distillery used to be. Where a lot of things used to be. Right on 3rd. A flash of red comes out of a side street. Harlow. She's ahead tonight. Not for long. I pick up the pace, shifting my weight forward, and push more power through the pedals. Tattered zebra-stripe bar tape slides beneath my palms, but that won't stop me catching up with her. Gaining on her from behind, I take a moment to admire the definition of her calves. Girl's got form.

"Hey, loser."

She whips round to face me, a wisp of red hair catching in the corner of her mouth. She's wearing lipstick tonight, and I fight back the thought of licking it off. No time for daydreaming. We've got a job to do.

"Alvarez," she grins, backing off the pace just a bit to let me slide in next to her. "What's a girl like you doing in a shitheap like this?" Her voice is breathy. Somehow those lungs of hers are still functioning.

"Heard this was an up-and-coming neighborhood."

She lets out a chuckle while dodging a dismembered car door with the reflexes of a rattlesnake. I veer away from scattered glass just in time to avoid shredding my tires, and we take a left on Salmon Street into The Black. This part of the grid blew years ago and no one bothered to repair it. That's fine. I've ridden through these shadows enough to know the way, and there's already a hint of flickering candlelight in a distant window. The others must be there already.

I spot Savannah's cargo bike as we throw our fixies down out front. We climb through the side window, into the old warehouse, with its long-neglected machinery coated in dust.

Harlow's rustling something in her jacket pocket that catches my attention. I grab her arm, pulling her closer.

"Open your mouth." She grins.

"I thought you'd never . . ."

Something hard hits my tongue and a burst of citrus sets my teeth on edge. I suck on the lollipop and give Harlow's hand a squeeze, hiding my delusional disappointment. Her skin's cold and clammy.

Savannah and Jonesy are in the back office, illuminated by candles.

"Evenin', fellas," Harlow chirps. She plucks the lollipop from my mouth and pops it into her own. I hate how much it turns me on.

No one gets up on our account, but they clock us as we enter. Savannah, naturally, is the first to speak.

"You're late."

I shrug. "Banks isn't here yet."

"Where are they?" Harlow nestles on what was once a sofa cushion on the floor.

"Getting dinner."

A twinge in my gut. I don't think I'll ever get used to that side of things.

"Did you bring it?" Savannah thrusts a hand in my direction, strawberry blond pigtails whipping her cheeks. She has the ragged, splintered palm of someone who recently clawed their way out of a coffin.

I hand over a sheet of paper before dropping to the floor next to Harlow and stealing the lollipop back. Since it's best not to give all my attention to the devastatingly attractive straight girl next to me,

I focus on the other two as they huddle together and scrutinize my first attempt at a makeshift flyer.

They're the powerhouses behind Rebel Dispatch, this gang of unruly undead teens hellbent on taking over the city. Savannah's the ideas girl and natural leader, with an endless supply of plans up her sleeve. I've known her since we were in kindergarten and she's always been a hardass. Don't let the cutesy appearance fool you.

Meanwhile Jonesy's got more energy than the rest of us combined. She's been riding hill reps for the past few weeks. Says she's training for Portland Heights. She can't wait to torment all those rich folks who think they're safe up there.

"This is good, Alvarez." Savannah bobs her head in approval, and I return a nod of thanks. "I love this part." She points at a section and sits back in her chair, resting a foot on the opposite knee. She quotes me. "*Too long have we wasted away in their shadow, out of sight, out of mind. They've had the monopoly for millennia and left us with nothing but the charred remains of a world they destroyed. It's time to rise and take it back, while there's still something worth fighting for.*" Pride warms my cheeks a little.

"Yeah, that's great." Jonesy's deep in thought and chewing the side of her thumb, right along the edge of where her cuticle should be. Losing the fingernails may have been the hardest part. That, and the change of menu.

"Okay." Savannah stands and pulls open the double doors to the warehouse. "Jonesy and I hit up some of the old studios on Broadway and found something pretty special."

We all grab a candle and follow. She leads us to a tabletop contraption with a bunch of movable plates, dials and letter stamps.

"Is that a printing press?" I beeline for the machine and pick up handfuls of letters with childlike excitement.

"I knew you'd love it," Savannah beams at me.

It takes us a while to figure out how to use it, and even longer to produce enough copies of my flyer, but it's a magical feeling when it's done. By midnight, we're shoving fistfuls of paper into our messenger bags.

"Who's taking what?"

Jonesy's arm shoots up, "The Heights."

We all laugh, like anyone expected anything else. She has this smug grin plastered across her face, and I'm stoked to see her hard work pay off. The girl's got mad muscle definition now. With her blond afro pixie resembling flames in the candlelight, and the warm tone of her dark skin staving off the deathly gray tinge of decay, she's glowing. Who knew you could start living your best life after death?

Banks bursts through the door, trudges over to us and wordlessly throws a damp-looking sack onto the floor. It lands with a flump that turns my stomach, filling the room with the metallic scent of a fresh kill. Savannah and Jonesy glance over at it with a sullen nod. Harlow offers a tense fist bump to Banks. The three of us hesitate as Banks reaches into the sack and pulls out something stringy. Swallowing back bile, I try to ignore the rumbling of my stomach for a little while longer.

Harlow gives in first. I sneak a look at her as she scoots tentatively past me towards dinner. She takes her time, steeling herself, then selects something fleshy and sidles over to Banks.

"Thanks," she says. They nod in response.

The two of them side by side is a sight to behold. Banks has always been the quiet one, but they're a presence nonetheless, standing almost six feet tall, muscular with the soft, round edges of residual puppy fat. The caretaker: primed for battle, but making sure we're fed first. When Banks is around, you can guarantee there's some poor fuck lying in a back alley somewhere with their skull cracked open.

Harlow on the other hand is tiny, around five-two, but perfectly proportioned. Beautiful. Deadly. Always had this uncanny ability to see the other side and commune with the dead. She's the one who brought us back when we carried out the pact.

"So, everyone knows their route tonight." Savannah reaches into Banks' bag of culinary horrors and retrieves a handful of innards. Coagulated blood trickles down her arm and chin as she forces it in. No one enjoys it but we need our strength, and it's the only thing that, somehow, stays down. With everyone partaking around me, I can't fight the hunger anymore. Gaze averted, I reach into the bag and try not to wretch when my fingers brush wet organs that are somehow still warm. Teeth fighting through the sinews, my brain screams in repulsion while the rest of my body collapses into the cravings like a ravenous feral dog.

Stomachs full, flyers made, and game plan in place, Jonesy huffs out the candles and we head to the street. We mount our bikes, moonlit and full of purpose, say goodnight, and begin the midnight paper route. Savannah and Jonesy head west, across the Hawthorne Bridge toward the old town. Banks throws a salute our way as they pedal in the direction of Sunnyside, and I reluctantly leave Harlow at the Lone Fir Cemetery. Tonight I'm hitting up Irvington, where there've been a lot of reports of poltergeist activity lately. We're not the only ones losing patience with the living, it seems. The dead have nothing but time on their hands. Of course we get restless.

Tillamook Street is wide, devoid of the maple trees that used to line it, just like the others. Ghostly faces peer down at me from several windows. They know something's stirring. I hold up a flyer for them to see, before slipping it through the door. One by one, I hear the metallic clatter of mailboxes shutting behind me, the flyers reaching their intended recipients. It takes a few hours to cover the whole Irvington area, and the sky's a dusty pink by the time I'm done.

Home these days is an abandoned motel on Interstate Avenue. This whole area was evacuated after an earthquake hit and the Willamette flooded, but the motel was spared and I like the peace and quiet. I've spotted a few stragglers around here, but the Monticello has been left mercifully alone. Initially Savannah suggested living together and having a Rebel Dispatch HQ, but we decided we needed our own space or we'd end up wanting to kill each other: a frustrating thought when you're already dead. I crawl into bed, the sun blocked out by boarded-up windows, and while I'm not sure why my body needs sleep, I'm not resisting its pull.

When I wake up I immediately think of Harlow. I've got it bad. Always had a crush on her when we were alive but in death, seeing her in action, everything intensified. It's becoming a problem; I can't be that friend who secretly leers. She trusts me. Somehow, despite our obvious flirtation and the fact she's known about my sexuality for a few years, she's never cottoned onto my feelings for her. I picture Harlow in her own sanctuary over in Rose City Park, holed up in an abandoned post office building with a bunch of other misfits. As if on cue, there's a knock at my door. She's standing outside.

"Hey."

"What are you doing here? The meeting doesn't start for another couple hours."

She flops down on the edge of my bed and looks up at me with big, doe eyes that set my head spinning. I bite the inside of my cheek. Keep it together.

"I need to talk."

"Okay." I land cross-legged next to her.

She nibbles her bottom lip and ties my stomach in knots. My mind's racing with all the possibilities, and of course at the forefront is this pointless hope that she's about to say she's realized the errors of her straight ways, and confess her love for me.

"I think we should call off the attack."

"That's not funny."

She rings her hands in her lap; my shoulders tighten in response.

"I'm serious. I don't want to do this."

Every time I have a sentence on the tip of my tongue it fizzles and melts away, and I realize I've not responded yet. Her brown eyes bore into me and it would feel good if it wasn't so terrifying. This girl, who chickened out of our pact at the last minute and brought us back into a whole new world, now wants out of it?

"But you're the reason we're here."

"They're not some distant aliens that mean nothing to us, Alvarez. They were our people once." As soon as I open my mouth to counter, she cuts me off. "It feels like a betrayal."

I turn away from her and we sit in silence for a moment. Running through all the possible ways this can go, what scares me most is imagining Savannah's reaction if she hears about this. The wrath it would bring.

"Okay, listen. I get that it's hard." She's not looking at me anymore. "But you know as well as I do that this is the only way for us to live, to be able to walk the streets. If they knew about us, you know they'd jump straight to violence. We're just beating them to it. They had their chance, Harlow. They're basically doomed anyway. We have to reclaim the city for ourselves."

"Are they doomed because of their actions, or ours?"

"They're the reason this city, this planet, is on its knees. They saw the apocalypse coming and they still drilled for oil."

"Are those people out there, in this city, right this minute, the reason the planet is dying?"

"But it's not about them, it's what they stand for. They had a monopoly on this world and they destroyed it. They don't deserve to keep it."

She crosses her arms and her whole body seems to hunch beneath the weight on her shoulders.

"And you think killing all those people is the answer?"

"I think we have as much a right to this city as they do, and they're not going to live peacefully alongside us."

"Well," she finally looks at me. "If we slaughter them all in the middle of the night, I guess we'll never know."

The silence drags after that, so I haul myself up off the bed and throw on some ripped jeans before sliding on my worn-out high tops. I grab my messenger bag, tie my hair into a ponytail and only then do I turn back to look at her. She's not moved at all.

"Listen," I fold my arms and shift my weight onto one foot. "I can't convince you, but you know that Savannah will lose her shit if she hears you talking like this. So either you're in, and you come to the meeting, or you're out, and you hide."

She looks up at me, and the conflict on her face tears me up inside, so I beeline for the door. She needs to see sense and come with me. I hover outside the motel until she finally emerges, saying nothing. I guess she's back on board when she picks up her bike and matches my pace all the way to the cemetery.

We ride through the darkness towards the huge mausoleum in the center, where we told everyone to meet. There's already a gathering, and though it's not quite as big as I'd imagined, it all sinks in that this is really happening. Around me are perhaps fifty faces, their old lives long since gone, but their bodies still very much kicking. We filter through the crowd, catching glimpses of graying skin and rotting limbs. We're definitely among our peers now.

The others are at the front, next to a pile of displaced gravestones forming a makeshift stage. Savannah greets us with wide-eyed excitement.

"Can you believe this?" She takes hold of my hands and gives them a squeeze. "Nice work on the flyers, Alvarez."

"Thanks." I glance nervously over at Harlow, who is hiding her misgivings remarkably well. She pats Jonesy on the shoulder and nods at Banks, before leaning against an iron fence and crossing her arms. *Just keep your mouth shut, please.*

After some excited bustling, Savannah hops up onto the rubble. She's getting straight on with the speech she prepared, but it's not without its disruptions. First some heckler calls her "just a kid," before he's sent shuffling away with a broken finger, and then there's more scuffling and shouting, before someone shoves a man towards the front. The first thing I notice is how hairy he is, with his shaggy mullet, scraggly beard, and a tuft of thick chest hair poking up through the collar of his check shirt. The second thing I notice, with a shock, is that this dude is very much alive.

"What the hell are you doing here?" Savannah's cool drains away and her hackles are raised. The crowd heckles. *He doesn't belong here. He's a spy. Kill him.*

The man raises his palms and lowers his head.

"I can explain," he shouts. "I promise, I'm one of you."

"That pink skin of yours says otherwise." Savannah shoots a look towards Banks, who takes a hulking step forward. The guy kneels.

"No," he pleads. "You're right, I'm alive, sort of. I know I look like them right now, but I swear, every month when the moon is full, I am one of you."

Savannah eyes him up and down, taking in the downy hair that covers his arms and his pointy, lupine features. I note his long fingernails with an unexpected pang of envy, and as though we're all joined telepathically, the group settles.

"Are there more of you?"

He nods. "They were too afraid to come."

"Bring them next time."

Word travels through the crowd. We want more on our side, not less. Banks retreats at Savannah's signal, and we're back to business. I scan faces, struck by the variety. A coven of witches stands a few rows back, alongside vampires, undead folks of all colors and creeds, and some sallow-skinned women in bedraggled white dresses.

"Portland has banshees?"

Harlow smirks at my disbelief.

"Portland is one of the last cities standing. It has *everything*."

Once Savannah's riled up the crowd, and everyone's nodding in furious agreement that yes, the humans have got to yield, she opens the floor for others to speak. Some are afraid to get their hands dirty, and they're shamed into getting over it. There's unanimity from the crowd that we're all ready to win this fight. Unless you count Harlow, who's carefully staying quiet next to me.

A few figures come forward, their graying flesh so translucent I can see faces through their limbs as they gesticulate. They inform us that ghosts are tied to their dwellings, so many can't attend our meetings. Savannah tasks me with writing a list of actions for furthering the movement within the confines of their homes. We'll distribute them later. The meeting's called to a close, with everyone instructed to spread the word and bring more folks to the next one.

Weeks go by, and the movement grows. The crowds get larger with each gathering, and finally we agree to make our move on the next full moon. War is declared. Responsibilities drawn up. Right now we're focusing on intel gathering and growing our army. The werewolves, who now attend in droves, blend in during daylight hours while the vampires seamlessly infiltrate underground parties at night. The bloodthirsty recruit, by any means necessary. The rest will play to their strengths later.

As for us, we're keeping up momentum, delivering messages to our incorporeal allies, and recruiting bikers for nightly training rides. There's no shortage of bikes abandoned around the city, and we're gonna need riders to herd the sheep.

A week before the full moon, after the final meeting, Harlow pulls Savannah aside. Jonesy's amped and joking with Banks about needing a full-on feast before the action, but my eyes are trained on the other two. Harlow's been off lately. I don't think the others have noticed, since they're so wrapped up in battle plans, but she's been receding into herself. She's not really hanging out with the other witches anymore, who are busy preparing explosives for next week. I watch them talking and gulp back the nausea. She's hunched over, arms folded, while Savannah's gradually tensing. This can't be good. I laugh at whatever Jonesy just said, tentatively step away, and glance over at Savannah just in time to see her grab Harlow by the throat. Launching towards them, I hear Savannah saying coldly: "You did your job. We don't need you anymore."

"Stop." I put a hand on her shoulder.

She doesn't break eye contact with Harlow. "If she's not with us then she's against us."

"Of course she's with us," I say. "She's just scared." She retracts her arm and pins Harlow with an icy stare before walking away. Jonesy and Banks keep their eyes lowered as they follow her.

We ride in silence together, bags full of flyers, until it's time to part. Harlow asks if she can come back to my place after rounds. A few hours later, I swallow the lump in my throat and watch her collapse into my bed.

"I swear she wasn't always that scary." She rubs her neck, and I instinctively touch my own.

I distract myself, picking up clothing from the floor and feeling like a slob. Once you've scratched your way through wood and crawled out of your own grave, tidying seems pointless. I accidentally kick her bag and flyers spill out of the opening.

"You didn't deliver them?"

She shifts on the bed, avoiding my glare.

"I don't think we should do this."

Not this again.

Now she sits up and looks me in the eye. "You've seen the way Savannah's acting. I thought this was a good idea at first but we're talking about innocent people's lives."

"Innocent?"

"Yeah, they're not the generation that fucked up the planet."

I lower myself to the edge of the bed, back turned to her to hide my disappointment.

"Huh."

"Alvarez, the people out there now, they're not to blame. They've been dumped with this mess just like us. Our families didn't bring about the apocalypse, did they? But you want to punish them, too?"

"We can't exactly go back in time to dole out the punishment to those who did though, can we?"

"And this is better?" She shifts towards me on the bed, gently placing a hand in mine. I'm trying so hard not to let my crush on her cloud my judgment.

"But we have to do something." I face her now, taking in the smoothness of her skin, her huge brown eyes, and that red hair of hers. She's achingly beautiful.

"Do we?" She squeezes my hand.

"What's the alternative? We just hide away in the shadows? They'll never let us coexist with them."

"We don't even know that. We've never tried."

I let her words hang in the air for a moment, unsure how to respond.

"It's my fault," she says. "I did this to us. I chickened out of death and brought us back, and now we're in this mess."

"Hey." I nudge her with my elbow. "I'm glad you brought us back."

"But all this power? Taking over the city? We're just kids, Alvarez."

I chew on my bottom lip, wondering if this building anger is at her for backing out of the plan, or at myself for wondering if she's right.

"Alvarez," her voice softens to almost a whisper. "Our families are still out there. My mom doesn't deserve to get caught up in this."

I open my mouth to respond, but she cuts me short.

"And neither does yours."

No sleep that night. I stay rigid on my back, arms folded so I don't accidentally brush against her. The excitement of us sharing a bed for the first time is muddled with the nagging thought that maybe she's right. I cast my mind back to what feels like years ago, but has probably only been a couple of months. Walking through the front door of my childhood home, fingers bleeding, palms covered in splinters, coated in ashes and dust. I felt the grief as I crossed the threshold, filling the air with a heaviness that enveloped me the way I hoped their arms would. In a way that they never would again.

As soon as Mom clocked me standing in the hallway, her eyes shot wide open, and the sounds that came from her reminded me of the dying pigs from the abattoir near abuelita's house. The sound of fear, of death. Instead of throwing her arms around me in relief, she threw them around my brother and dragged him back through the kitchen, screaming for my father to come. I knew right then, I didn't want him to see me. I didn't belong there anymore.

I try to think further back, to when we were happy. I'd always had this sense of foreboding, like the world we inhabited wasn't real, that we were living on borrowed time. Even when I was small, I was vaguely aware of a wasteland in a place called 'out there,' and that humans had been the earth's undoing. But in hindsight, tonight in this bed with Harlow sleeping next to me, I also remember something else. My parents, while trying to be strong for us, would give off small signals that they were just as afraid as we were. The hushed but frantic whispers behind closed doors, and the muffled crying. Mom's eyes shining and blinking hard when Tomas asked what happened to the trees in his picture books.

It wasn't their fault. As much as I want to cling to my anger, to have someone to blame, and to set the world to right, I can't deny it anymore. While I'm not prepared to give up the fight and a claim to life here in the city, I don't want my family to suffer. In the morning, I tell Harlow that I'll help her warn the people we love, and then she needs to disappear.

With only a few days until the full moon, Harlow and I hatch a plan. We skip our daytime rest to sneak back to the warehouse and create a new flyer. This one carries a warning of the impending attack: when to stay off the streets, the timings of our movements, and the locations we'll use as key battlegrounds. We deliver them to our families and pray they heed our words.

When we're done, we go back to her place to gather her things. Her room's much neater than mine, glittering with crystals and geodes. Back outside, I watch helplessly as she mounts her bike, an oversized duffel bag slung over her shoulder. She grabs my arm and pulls me close.

"Come with me," Harlow pleads.

God, I wish I could.

"I need to do this, and you have to leave the city before Savannah gets her hands on you."

Her eyes glisten, skin kissed by the golden hour sun. The thought of never seeing her again kills me a second time.

"But—"

The silence hovers between us. I take her hands in my own. Saying goodbye to the first girl I fell in love with, it's finally time to be honest.

"You know how I feel about you, right?"

Her eyes dart from left to right, taking in the full force of my stare, charged with pointless hope. It dissipates when she lowers them.

"I'm not—"

"I know. It's okay."

She meets my eyes once more, tears finally escaping. I squeeze her tight, breathing in the last of her, before turning my back so I don't have to watch her ride away.

On the night of the full moon, the Lone Fir Cemetery crowd is the biggest it's ever been. They're spilling out onto the surrounding streets, and it takes us way too long to reach the mausoleum. The recruitment drive must have worked, though I'll never understand why so many people freshly turned are willing to fight for our side. I guess they don't have a choice in the matter.

Savannah's voice projects from a tinny megaphone. By the time I reach her, she's screaming encouragement and riling up the crowd. Jonesy and Banks nod along fervently. They hadn't taken Harlow's departure lightly, but thankfully they knew it was pointless to go after her.

There's a thirst for blood in the air tonight. When it's go-time Savannah and Jonesy lead the charge, and as everyone moves out, I allow myself one last thought of Harlow, before putting my war head on. We're assigned our cohorts, and I roll out towards Irvington once more, this time flanked by hundreds of undead bikers. Upon arriving, we fan out into smaller groups and cover as much of the area as possible, awaiting the cue to move to the next phase.

It's not long until muffled screams come from several houses close by. Lights flicker, windows open and slam shut, there's the crashing of breaking glass and banging doors, and I catch glimpses of flying objects and residents clambering from one room to the next in their nightwear. All around me, the ghostfolk are upholding their end of the deal, terrorizing people until, at last, they begin to spill out onto the streets. I wait a few minutes, allowing more of them to congregate in the road, shrieking towards their neighbors and lamenting their rude midnight awakening. Once it feels like most of them are out, and the crowd hysteria is reaching its peak, I let out a sharp whistle and we close in. At first they don't understand what's happening, but the sight of a horde of bikers headed straight for them, hooting and hollering, is enough to rattle them into running in the opposite direction.

The game's afoot. We herd them like sheep, nipping at their ankles with our front wheels and chasing them down the hill towards the designated carnage zones where they'll find the rest of our number lying in wait. In the distance there's a muffled thud of explosives being lobbed at high-rise buildings, and the air is filled with the metallic tang of blood. Something stirs in me. Perhaps it's sheer adrenaline, or maybe something more. All I know is I'm riding on a high and the chaos around me is electrifying. Out of every side street pours more of our army, entering the battlefield with tooth and claw, feeding the frenzy.

I wish Harlow were here to see this, and then immediately dismiss the thought. Thinking of her is enough to dissipate some of the ecstasy, to take in some of the faces in the crowd, and momentarily stop dead in my tracks. A flash of big, brown eyes, a mop of thick, curly dark hair, and what I'm sure is a walnut-sized birthmark on the side of a neck. Was that Tomas? As quickly as the image of my baby brother appears, it's gone, and I'm filled with doubt. Of course it wasn't him, I warned my family to leave the city ahead of tonight. And yet, who's to say that they believed me? Where would they even go?

It's like the wind's knocked out of me, and suddenly I'm gasping for air I don't need, but it's a reflex from the memory of being alive and oh god, oh god, what if they're here? What if we failed, and the only living people I love in this world are being trampled by a horde of monsters? I falter a little, meandering through the crowd towards the outskirts before shifting a foot to the rear tire to ease myself to a standstill. Suddenly the good feeling's gone, and I swallow the panic rising up from my stomach. They're out there. I can feel it.

"Alvarez!"

I look up through the crowd and spot Savannah, pushing her way through towards me. Her blond pigtails and porcelain skin are spattered red and there's a wild look on her face that genuinely frightens me.

"Hey," I mumble as she slaps a firm grasp on my shoulder.

"Isn't this insane?" she clucks, wide-eyed and ecstatic.

"It—yeah."

"What's wrong?"

I study her for a moment, hoping to soak up some of that excitement and get back to the good place. Instead I feel sick, and decide to buy myself some time to recover. For the rest of the night I hold position near the back, eventually pushing through the fear and recovering some of the thrill I'd felt before. It must have been my imagination, there's no way Tomas would have been in the crowd. My folks wouldn't have ignored the warning. Still, I try not to focus on any individual faces in the crowd and detach myself from my surroundings as much as possible. I'm thankful that my main role in all this is circling the battlefield and preventing any stragglers from escaping, and that the bloodshed is someone else's job.

The dusty pink of a dawn sky creeps its way sleepily over the horizon, and the exhaustion finally hits me. I send my fixie clattering to the ground and stumble away from the last remaining fighters still somehow clambering to overpower each other. We've been running on fumes all night, and now the rising sun paints the city—our battleground—in a harsh and unforgiving glow. With every muscle in my body screaming in unison, I trundle through the streets, each step heavier than the last, and vaguely become aware that Savannah, Banks, and Jonesy are at my side. No one says a word. Gradually the air, thick with the spray of blood and the dying cries of the doomed, thins with the brightness of the morning sun.

For the first time, I really look around, and allow myself to take it all in. I'm not sure exactly in what order I notice all the details. Perhaps I start with the big things, like the leveled buildings, now piles of rubble surrounded by the shattered glass of blown out windows. Maybe it's the eerie silence around us, and the total lack of movement from anyone other than ourselves. Not a single sign of life.

My brain's working at fifty miles an hour, taking in as much as possible. Dusty faces, open eyes, sticky blood stains on the tarmac, dismembered limbs. We slowly head in the direction of the Willamette, and the body count keeps rising. We're not keeping tabs, but it's hard not to have a vivid sense of how many dead bodies are around you at one time.

Instinctively, I wander over to a destroyed building to my right, pulled by a sense of needing to bear witness. I taste bile as I spot the limp, tattooed arm of a woman jutting out of the rubble. Her body is pressed between a floor and ceiling, now unexpectedly united. Dried patches of blood spatter the black ink on her pale, dusty skin, and to my relief her face is concealed behind a chunk of concrete. Just to the right, a small square of yellow paper dangling from some string catches my eye, fluttering about in the wind. It's a tea bag, just a few feet away from her.

"Come on," Savannah pulls me away.

We walk through it all, and decide to cross Hawthorne Bridge to the old town. It's exactly the same. Bodies everywhere. The blood, guts and gore of humans and monsters alike. The whole city is still. The four of us, walking instead of wheeling, for once, forced to reckon with our actions, with a question on our lips that no one is brave enough to ask aloud.

I take a long look at them, my oldest friends, with whom I've literally gone to the other side and come back again, and my mind turns to Harlow. Against all odds, I cannot help but wonder if there's time to catch her up before she's truly gone for good.

WHEN IT'S OVER

SIRI CALDWELL

There was broken glass on the bridge.

Again.

Scarlett feathered her bicycle's brakes and hoped she could avoid the glass, but there was only so much swerving she could do—not with traffic breathing down her neck, drivers asserting their God-given right to crowd bicyclists off the road, and a rusty guardrail too low to stop anyone from toppling into the river.

She knew she was supposed to be assertive and own the travel lane instead of allowing herself to be trapped in the narrow, unsafe gutter that collected the road's grit and debris. She was supposed to think it was her fault she didn't have the guts to demand respect from two-ton vehicles. She *did* feel like it was her fault, she did, she couldn't help it. She blamed herself for not doing better, for not trying harder, for being a wimp, for being wrong—rather than blaming a car-centric society unwilling to build protected bike lanes that would give everyone room to breathe.

The puddle of beer-bottle-brown glass shards glittered angrily in the angled morning sun. Her fingers hovered over the brakes. Would it help to slow down? Or speed up? She'd loved high school physics (even her soon-to-be girlfriend fidgeting in the front row adjusting her high ponytail hadn't managed to distract her . . . much . . .), but had they learned this? Wheels versus sharp objects? The crucial factor should be how much weight pressed down, and that was a vertical force, while her velocity was horizontal, which would not affect a vertical force, and yikes, here she was. She steadied her handlebars and rode over the hazard with a sickening crunch.

Nothing popped or hissed, but a little way past the end of the bridge, she felt a change. She dismounted to check her front tire. It was flat.

Again.

She was going to be late for work.

Again.

She carried her bike off the road into the scraggly weeds, sidestepped a forlorn hubcap, and found a spot to lay her bike on its side. She popped the quick-release to remove the front wheel, ran her gloved palm over the tire to be sure there wasn't any glass embedded in the tread, and settled on the ground with her tire iron to work the tire off the rim. Car exhaust blew in her face.

"Scarlett! What are you doing here?"

Scarlett startled. Coughed. She'd know that voice anywhere. It was hoarser than back when they'd dated, but it was unmistakably Giselle. Almost as if thinking about her and her ponytail had conjured her up. When was the last time she'd allowed herself to remember how obsessed they'd been in high school? Not recently, that was for sure. You didn't survive a breakup after eight years of being inseparable by picking at the scab. She had moved on.

Acutely aware she was sitting in dirt, Scarlett squinted up at her.

Giselle's candy-red-lipsticked mouth was stretched into a delighted smile, her arms open for a hug. Like that was a thing they did.

Not anymore, they didn't.

"I don't do hugs."

Giselle gave a wounded laugh. Her arms dropped awkwardly to her sides. "Not even with me?"

"You broke up with me, remember?"

"So now I have cooties like everyone else?"

"Sure do," Scarlett said, which was rude, but she was in no mood to restart an old argument or justify herself to someone who'd claimed to love her despite having never believed Scarlett was good enough. She removed the wheel's tube and inspected the inside of the tire for problems.

"It's been ages," Giselle said, apparently unbothered by Scarlett's unenthusiastic welcome. There'd been a time when Scarlett had liked that about her, her unwillingness to take offense.

"I guess we were bound to run into each other at some point." If Giselle still lived in their old apartment—certainly a possibility—it was lucky they hadn't crossed paths before now.

"I saw you as I was driving by. I wanted to make sure you didn't need help." Giselle gestured like she was offering to squeeze her bike into the back of her little Nissan Versa and give her a ride. The rumble of traffic meant Scarlett hadn't heard her pull onto the shoulder, but there her car was, hazard lights blinking. The flirtatious pink eyelashes adorning the headlights were new.

"Um . . ." Were they the type of exes who cut off all contact but made an exception for roadside assistance? "Thanks. I've got it under control."

"I drive this way to work. I pass you on your bike sometimes, but I can't honk or yell out the window, 'cause I remember you used to complain about people doing that and giving you a heart attack."

She would've preferred not to know that.

"Do you . . ." Giselle hesitated, and Scarlett's mind filled in the blanks. *Do you want to have dinner? Do you ever wish things had been different? Do you have someone new?* "Do you ever see me driving by?"

Scarlett almost laughed with relief. "Sorry. I don't really pay attention unless a vehicle's being a jerk."

Giselle's smile returned. "So the fact that you didn't notice me is a compliment."

"I guess."

"Don't hurt yourself gushing about how wonderful I am."

Scarlett sighed. Had Giselle always been so exhausting? Always pushing, always needing Scarlett's full attention?

"You really didn't see me?"

"I don't know that I'd recognize your car without that bumper sticker." The JUST SAY NO TO GENDER ROLES sticker had been an anniversary gift from Scarlett, and when Giselle stuck it on, all gluey and a pain in the ass to remove, it felt like a declaration. A commitment. A hint she wanted to make things permanent.

"The sticker's still there."

"You didn't scrape it off?" She'd assumed Giselle wouldn't have kept a daily reminder of a person she didn't want anymore.

"I like it."

She wasn't going to ask if Giselle felt a sentimental attachment to it—to their relationship—or if the implication was that, for her, the sticker had never been about the two of them at all.

Giselle slid her hands in her pockets. "I still think about you, you know."

"About how terrible we were together?"

"We had good days," Giselle protested.

Scarlett tried not to think about their good days. "I guess."

"I know things didn't end well, but can you at least tell me you don't hate me?"

"I don't hate you." She set the tire down since it was obvious she wasn't going to get anything done until Giselle finished reminiscing and took off. "You did us a favor, ending things. We're better off apart. You just saw it sooner than I did."

"You're at peace with it? With what I did to you?"

"You didn't do anything to me." Giselle didn't have to make it sound like Scarlett was a victim. They'd both been hurting, and Giselle had done what needed to be done. It had taken Scarlett a while to understand that, but by now . . . yeah. She got it. "It was just . . . life."

Giselle looked relieved. Lighter, somehow. "Hug?"

Scarlett huffed in amusement at Giselle's dogged determination to get what she wanted. "There's this concept you might have heard of," she said. "Personal space."

Giselle laughed, but she kept her distance and didn't try to touch her. "You're so predictable."

Just for that, Scarlett pushed herself to her feet and opened her arms to pull her into one last hug while she remembered why she'd once loved her.

Her arms passed through her—through air—through Giselle's suddenly fading, ghostly form.

Scarlett stumbled.

What the . . . ?

Giselle pressed her hands over her heart, then pointed over Scarlett's shoulder in the direction of the bridge.

Scarlett didn't want to turn her back to her, but panic made her snap around. The air shimmered. Time unspooled on two overlapping, offset reels. Superimposed over the steady stream of traffic, a ghostly Nissan Versa and a garbage truck crashed into each other, sending the lighter vehicle airborne. It hit the top of the guardrail, its JUST SAY NO TO GENDER ROLES sticker clearly visible, defiant to the last.

Scarlett's head filled with static. Her legs gave out. She sank to the ground.

The Versa tumbled over the edge. Soundlessly, it hit the water.

Scarlett looked back over her shoulder.

Giselle was gone.

Dead Boy's Hill

Kay Hanifen

I stood in my seat, my legs burning as I pumped my pedals up the bicycle path of Dead Boy's Hill. Even though I could feel the familiar tickle of exercise-induced asthma attack, as my breaths became wheezes, I didn't let the guys down below hear me. They already had plenty of reasons to tease the weird fat girl; they didn't need more.

To be honest, I didn't know what Elise saw in them, aside from their popularity. But she'd turned into a swan over the summer while I stayed the ugly duckling, and now everyone wanted to be her friend. Or something more. I saw the way that Kaelan and Jared looked at her, and she seemed to be enjoying the attention. Did she even like them, though?

Attraction and crushes always seemed fake to me. I guess that people would call me asexual, but I just call myself an island of sanity amid a roiling ocean of hormones. Sure, maybe I'd like a girlfriend someday, but there wasn't anyone who made my heart flutter like it's supposed to. Maybe Elise thought that this would be a good double date—me and Kaelan, her and Jared. I hadn't told her, yet, that I prefer girls to guys. Or that I'm not interested in anyone in that way at the moment.

Still, I guess I'm supposed to be grateful that she wanted to include me at all, but being around the three of them made me feel like I was on the outside of a joke that everyone else seemed to be in on.

So, here I was on Halloween night, pedaling up the sixty-degree angle of Dead Boy's Hill in my Bride of Frankenstein costume, refusing to concede to the growing wheeze in my breath and take a break, when I should have been at home with Elise eating candy and having a scary movie night with my dad. But he was gone—my first Halloween without him—and she wanted to hang out with her new friends. It wasn't like I just invited myself along. She said I could come with her, and I knew that I didn't want to be alone.

Coughing, I took a moment to appreciate just how pathetic I felt. All this for a stupid dare.

Ten minutes ago, though it felt like hours, we all sat around a campfire at the base of Dead Boy's Hill drinking some beers that Kaelan stole, pretending that it didn't taste like piss. The flavor of teenage rebellion is much sweeter than that of beer, so we all do it.

Eventually, Jared cleared his throat, clinking on his glass bottle like he was about to give a toast. He was dressed in his brother's old football uniform, complete with the helmet. "Okay, everyone, we all know the story of Billy Barnes and Dead Boy's Hill, but in honor of tonight, the night he died, we'll tell it again."

I settled back against the lawn chair and considered grabbing another marshmallow to roast over the fire. I'd already had a couple s'mores and I didn't want to look too much like a pig.

"Billy Barnes was a big kid," Jared said. "A bit like Sparrow over there. No offense."

With a withering glare, I flipped him off. "Offense taken."

"Don't be a dick," Elise admonished him, throwing a marshmallow. It bounced harmlessly off his forehead, and he flashed her a shit-eating grin. She was dressed as a cat—cliché and classic.

"You're not funny." One hand already full with a marshmallow roasting over the fire, Kaelan dropped his fake pirate hook hand and dug in the bag, throwing another at him.

"Your mom thinks I'm hilarious." Jared cleared his throat, unconcerned. "Anyway, like I was saying. Billy Barnes was a big kid, and everyone else made fun of him for it. On Halloween night, while he was pigging out on all the candy he stole from younger neighborhood kids, the guys he was with made a bet. They said that Billy was too fat to ride his bike all the way up Dead Boy's Hill and then back down again. Billy accepted the challenge."

"You okay?" Elise whispered, seeing me shift uncomfortably in my seat.

"Fine." I didn't look her in the eye. I'd always hated this story.

"But his friends had a prank planned. So, while Billy was huffing and puffing his way up the hill, they set up a clothesline, planning to knock him off his bike when he came down at full speed. They made a mistake, though. Instead of having the line at chest level, it was as high as his throat. When Billy reached the top and came sailing back down, his bike going faster than it had ever gone before, he hit the clothesline at full speed."

At this, Jared paused for dramatic effect. "Billy's body and bike kept going for a few feet further before both toppled over, but his head flew backwards, bouncing off the bike path before rolling into the woods. His friends took one look at the bleeding stump and ran. A jogger found him the next morning, his body completely drained of blood and underneath his bicycle. But they never found the head."

He leaned in closer, the shadows of firelight flickering along his face. "Now, they say that if you try to ride up and down Dead Boy's Hill on Halloween Night, Billy will come looking for his head. And when he can't find it, he'll take yours instead." Straightening, he grinned. "So, any volunteers?"

We all fell silent, staring at each other. It wasn't that we believed a word of the Billy Barnes story, but we were tipsy and the idea of riding a bike up a stupidly tall hill sounded completely unappealing.

"Come on," he cajoled. And, of course, he then turned to me. "How about you, Sparrow? You look like you could use the exercise."

"And you look like a colossal asshole." I got to my feet as Kaelan and Elise *oohed*. "It's been . . . well, not exactly fun—sorry Elise and Kaelan—but I think I'm gonna go now."

Jared shot me a shit-eating grin. "What are you more scared of, Billy Barnes or the exercise?"

"Jared, shut up," Kaelan hissed.

"Yeah, what is your problem?" Elise's words were standing up for me, but her eyes looked like she pitied me and my pathetic retreat from that asshole.

I ignored him, grabbing my bike and shoving my wig in my backpack so that I could put on my helmet.

Jared, though, was undaunted. "Yeah, that's right. Go home and pig out on candy, have a heart attack like your dad."

Right. That was it. You can make fun of me all you want, but jokes about my dad could not stand. Not when the mere mention of him still pierced my heart with grief. Whipping around, I punched Jared in the face. Then, in a swift motion, I grabbed him by the shoulders and kneed him in the gut before sweeping his legs out from under him and knocking him to the ground. I may be fat, but I also just earned my black belt in Taekwondo. Technically, I shouldn't have used my skills unless I was in real physical danger, but the deep satisfaction I felt when he stared up at me shocked and wheezing was just too good for me to regret it.

Jared wiped some of the blood off his nose, smearing the crimson across his cheek like clown makeup. "The fuck is wrong with you?"

I shrugged. "I warned you. So, now let's make a deal. When I make it up and down Dead Boy's Hill, you have to explain to everyone who asks about your black eye that you got it by insulting someone's dead dad."

Elise grabbed my arm before I could mount the bike. "Sparrow."

"What?" I snapped. Maybe I shouldn't have blamed her, but in the moment, all I could think about was Halloweens from years past where we trick-or-treated or handed out candy while watching scary movies. That should have been this year. too, but she *had* to go out with boys instead.

"I'm sorry for dragging you along," she said. "I didn't know Jared would act like such an asshole tonight. You don't have anything to prove to him."

I sighed. "I get that you're pretty now, so everyone wants to pay attention to you and be your friend, or . . . you know. Just—just try to remember who's always had your back." With that, I mounted the bike and began to pedal up Dead Boy's Hill.

My heart raced as the cold air irritated my already irritated lungs and sweat droplets rolled down my face. After what had felt like hours, I reached the top. I made it. It was literally all downhill from here.

I paused, catching my breath as I stared down at the small fire below. In this chilly weather, the tickle in my throat likely wouldn't go away for hours. But it was worth it to prove Jared wrong, if nothing else.

I kicked off, pumping a little before the pedals were moving too fast for me to keep up. The wind whipped through my hair, and I was glad that I thought to put my wig in my bag. Even with the strongest spirit gum, it would have been torn away. I laughed in exhilaration, feeling like I was on a roller coaster.

As I neared the bottom, though, my bike jerked to a sudden stop, flipping me over the handlebars and sending me flying. I landed hard on the paved bike path. Bones crunched, tearing a scream from my lungs. And the world faded to darkness.

As I slowly returned to consciousness, I wondered if I was still in the world at all. Maybe the story of Billy Barnes was true, and I'd had my head chopped off by an invisible clothesline. But every inch of me hurt too much for me to not be attached to my body.

"What the fuck, Jared?" someone yelled, though it sounded like I was listening to the conversation from below the surface of a swimming pool.

"Oh God, is she dead?" another voice added to the mix. A familiar, feminine voice. I liked this one.

"It's fine. She's still breathing. We've all fallen from our bikes at some point. She probably has no idea what happened." That third and final voice was one that I hated. Somehow, I just knew that he was the one responsible for the pain I was in.

"She's awake," the feminine voice—Elise, it was Elise—said. She loomed over me, her shadow blocking out all the stars. "Sparrow. Sparrow, can you hear me?"

The best I could manage was a groan. Something bright invaded my eyes, making my head burst in a paroxysm of pain. "Stop."

"Sorry. I'll turn it off in a second. I just need to get a better look at your injuries." The light vanished. "We need to call 9-1-1."

"No way," said the voice I hated. Jared. Fucking Jared. "I'm the one who threw that football at her bike. My parents will kill me, especially if she sues. Hell, I could go to jail."

"Is she conscious enough to know what happened?" came the other boy's voice. Kaelan. I didn't hate the sound of his voice like Jared's, but I didn't love it like Elise's. I felt neutrally towards him, but depending on the next thing he said, my feelings could very easily become hatred.

"Does it matter?" Elise snapped. "I'm calling."

"No, you're fucking not." At the sounds of a scuffle, I turned my head. Jared and Elise were fighting over the phone while Kaelan watched, completely useless. My own phone was in my backpack, which I had placed in my bike basket before climbing the hill. If I could just reach . . .

Moving my arm made me white out with pain. Someone screamed—probably me, by the way my throat felt raw when the agony abated.

"That's it," Kaelan said, pulling his phone from his pocket and dialing it. "Hello? Hi, there's been an accident at the base of Dead Boy's Hill, and I think we need an ambulance."

"Kaelan, what the fuck?" Jared turned from Elise and barreled into him, tackling him to the ground. The phone skidded in the grass, and I could vaguely hear the tinny voice on the other end of the line as the boys tussled.

The hulking figure didn't so much emerge from the woods as he appeared like flicking on a light switch. One moment, it was the four of us. The next, someone had ripped Kaelan off Jared and held him one-handed in the air. Kaelan struggled against the stranger, elbowing him and knocking his head back.

It flopped like it was on a hinge, going completely upside down. White bone vertebrae buried in the stump of his neck glinted in the moonlight. Billy Barnes stared back at me, his head upside down and dangling against his back.

If it wasn't for the unnatural angle, he would have looked like any other guy in my class. His cherubic cheeks were smattered with acne and his eyes were soft, even as his face twisted in anger at the inconvenience of having his head nearly knocked off. He grabbed the blond hair on the crown of his head and set it back where it should have been. Then, he twisted Kaelan's neck, and with a sickening snap like the crunch of a twig, Kaelan went still.

With Kaelan dead, his attention was now on Jared, who had been lying on the ground, paralyzed with fear.

"Stay—stay the fuck away from me!" he cried, scrambling to his feet, and backing up. It was no use. Jared tried to run, but quick as a rattlesnake, Billy Barnes grabbed him and slammed him into a tree so hard that it shook several autumn leaves from their loose moorings. Jared let out an awful gurgling sound, but he wasn't dead. Not yet.

Billy Barnes stepped on his neck, slowly applying weight until it snapped. Then, he picked up Jared's inert body and began twisting, the bones breaking and muscles and tendons popping. With a wet, tearing sound the flesh ripped open, blood gushing from the wound.

He held Jared's head in one hand and his body in the other before tossing them aside and turning to me.

This was all my fault. If I hadn't risen to stupid Jared's stupid bait, none of this would have happened. I would be at home watching a scary movie, pretending that my dad was just in the other room, there to watch with me and make fun of the special effects. Kaelan and Jared would be alive, and I wouldn't be lying here broken and helpless. If there was one bright side to this, I guess, it would be that I'd be seeing Dad soon. *Sorry, Mom. I'll miss you.*

But something else was missing.

Elise. Where was Elise? I knew that I wouldn't be able to run like this—I could barely move—but Elise could get away. She *had* to get away.

As Billy Barnes approached, though, a shape stepped in front of me. Elise stood as a human shield with a burning log in her hand, brandishing it like a weapon. I wasn't sure what it would do, seeing as he was not a pack of wolves or anything living enough to fear fire, but to my surprise, Billy Barnes hesitated.

"If you want her, you'll have to go through me," she said.

He advanced again, more cautious this time. But then, like Moses and the Burning Bush, a voice seemed to emanate from the fire in her hands. "Not them, Billy. You've had your revenge." Though I hadn't heard it in months, it was still painfully familiar. I hoped that I would never forget it.

"Dad?" I croaked.

Elise dropped the burning log in shock.

Billy Barnes froze in his tracks. By his foot, the voice on Kaelan's phone was still speaking. "Hello? Hello, are you still there? We're tracing the call now, so please stay on the line." Help was coming. We just had to live long enough for them to arrive.

Dad spoke again, his voice coming from everywhere and nowhere. "Give them the phone, Billy, and let them be. You've done enough."

Hesitantly, Billy Barnes grabbed the phone. Holding it out in front of him like a dirty diaper, he offered it to Elise before turning and lumbering back into the forest.

She sagged to the ground beside me and took my hand. "I'm so sorry. About everything. For making you feel like I ditched you, and for dragging you out here with those dickheads, and for letting Jared throw that stupid football. We really should've stayed back to watch scary movies and hand out candy like you wanted all along. Can you ever forgive me?"

Despite the pain, I forced myself to shake my head. It sent the world spinning, and I had to take a second to collect myself. "No, I'm glad I came," I mumbled as the forest filled with the sounds of sirens and the flashing blue and red lights. A tear streaked down my cheek, and it wasn't from pain this time. "I got to hear my dad's voice again. And I won't give that up for the world."

THE HALLOWEEN UNDERGROUND

SUMMER JEWEL KEOWN

I should have known, when I swiped right and that happy little swish of a message popped right up, that something was off. *You have a match*! digitally shouted across my screen with an ebullience that vastly outstated its potential. And yet, it made me lean closer, ever hopeful, ever foolish. I glanced around my office to make sure no one could see me messing around on a dating app instead of working on the grant report that was almost overdue. No one was looking, most of them off prepping the conference room for our lunchtime pumpkin carving contest. My coworkers loved a team-building exercise, and Halloween was the perfect opportunity for the Fun Committee to hatch some organized fun.

It wasn't that I *never* got matches on the apps, but they were usually with someone whose profile had only merited a *meh, well, maybe?* from me in the first place and as soon as I actually matched I had instant swiper's remorse. The women I found actually attractive and interesting kept far out of my electronic ether. And so, I was resigned to keep trudging through that single life, which was honestly fine with me much of the time.

Delilah, though, was exactly my type. Or, rather, the type I'd always daydreamed about but never actually had the nerve to actually speak to, let alone ask out on a date. I immediately jumped back to her profile and swiped through her photos again, carefully parsing each word of her bio, since the first time around I wouldn't have wasted my time learning too much about a person who clearly would never deign to swipe right on someone like me.

Her Joan Jett-style dark hair with messy bangs fell artfully into her walnut-colored eyes, which were perfectly outlined in thick black eyeliner, cat-eyed at the edges. Her deep red lipstick, black leather jacket with roses embroidered on the lapels, art deco earrings: it all added up to immediately making me realize just how dull I was in comparison, with my dishwater brown hair and barely-average makeup skills. But still, if she was at all curious about me, for whatever reason, I knew I would muster every compelling thought I'd ever had and channel them in her direction.

I read back through my own profile, trying to imagine what impression it would have made when she read about me for the first time. Could I possibly seem cool? Did my awkwardness shine through my photos and the text I'd painstakingly revised over and over again to sound like I'd just thrown it together? I wondered if I should have deleted the line that said I loved cats, but other people's cats, since currently I didn't have any of my own. Was that boring? Delilah's profile said she had three cats, so maybe I sounded perfect. Or maybe she just needed a cat sitter while she traveled somewhere Insta-worthy with someone much more interesting than me.

I am aware that I have confidence issues, all right? I've tried therapy, I've tried self-help books and mantras and telling myself in the mirror that I am as great as or at least equal to sliced bread. I know I can sound like a total Eeyore. But the truth is that I'm really only down on myself when I see myself in comparison to much cooler people, and Delilah was definitely one of those.

In the midst of my spiral into insecurity, a message from Delilah popped up on my screen. I couldn't believe it. Matching was one thing, but I'd already assumed it would be one of those situations where I said hello, along with something mildly clever or quippy, which would then be followed by weeks of radio silence until I unmatched out of embarrassment. But an actual message meant she had intentionally swiped right on me and hadn't just twitched a finger in the wrong direction on accident. I opened the message, quickly, holding my breath.

"Happy Halloween!" it said. "How's your spooky holiday going? Had to pop in to say you've got great style—we might need to meet up just so I can steal the earrings in your third photo. LOL. Anyway, how has your day been so far?"

My heart pounded. This was really happening. I flipped back to my third photo, where I was wearing the oversize pink wooden earrings I'd impulse-purchased at a gift shop in Irvington. They were probably the coolest jewelry I owned. I thanked past me for buying them even though they were a little out of my comfort zone, and for taking the selfie even though selfies make me cringe. I begged my brain cells to be clever, quickly. Come on, Maia, let's get charming.

I typed a message, then deleted it, then typed and deleted again. Finally, I landed on, "You can borrow my earrings if I can borrow your jacket! Happy Halloween—getting ready for the office pumpkin carving contest. Any ideas for a winning design?"

Yeah, I thought, *that works*. I hit send before I could rethink myself into oblivion. Then I stared at my phone for way too long, just in case she immediately responded. But no, people like Delilah don't just watch their phones, waiting for messages. They're out doing things—important, interesting things—they're not attached to their devices with short electronic leashes like me.

It was about an hour later that another bubble popped up on my phone. This time we traded messages back and forth a few times in quick succession. She suggested I carve a monster truck or a wolf on my pumpkin. I asked her what her Halloween plans were. She told me she was going to Bike Social, and asked had I ever heard of it.

I had, and I'd even bookmarked posts about it a few times, but I didn't know anyone else who went, and the idea of going to a massive traveling bike gathering all by myself was always a little too much. A Halloween-themed ride sounded really cool, and I could imagine Delilah right in the thick of it, queen of spooky spokes.

If you don't have solid plans tonight, you should come with, she said.

My heart thump-thumped out of my chest, onto the floor, and down the hallway. I set a timer on my phone for eighteen minutes, then shoved it to the back of my desk drawer. I was absolutely going to say yes, but didn't want to sound overeager. I wanted her to think I was as cool as the Bike Social regulars. Little did I know that she absolutely did not care about that.

I took off work early, as soon as the pumpkin carving contest was complete and judged and my hissing cat pumpkin got an honorable mention, so that I could scare up some kind of bike-friendly Halloween costume. That led me to waiting by the City Market, with a witch's hat glued to my helmet, wearing a black T-shirt I'd ripped up and a whole lot of smudged black eyeliner, a broom zip-tied to my bike's frame. The plastic black raven I'd found at the picked-over Halloween store stood proudly on my handlebars. I hoped it was nonchalant enough but not apathetic.

Blood whooshed loudly through my veins as I watched the cyclists arrive across the street, exchanging hugs and intricate handshakes. Their costumes varied from minimal cat ears to Batman on a black bike, to someone who rolled up dressed as death, holding a big plastic scythe. A big part of me wanted to pedal the hell away as fast as I could. The idea of trying to puff myself up for the next few hours enough to impress a cute girl was overwhelming, let alone doing it in the middle of the cool kids bicycle club. But I imagined the pat on the back my former therapist would have given me for taking a chance, and I told myself to just fucking do this already.

Delilah rolled up right then on a fixed gear that was bright red with white stripes, blue accents inside its white wheels and a white wicker basket mounted on the handlebars. With anyone else it could have been a patriotic monstrosity but she made it look like the coolest bike that ever biked. She was dressed like Dorothy from *The Wizard of Oz*, only more punk rock, with black leggings underneath her blue and white gingham dress. Her hair was in two short braids, with little blue bows at each end. I imagined helping her undo them, her hair holding a slight wave as I separated the strands, and my core temperature rose. And the finishing touch, a little stuffed dog peeked out of her bike basket. Adorable.

She seemed to know everyone at Bike Social, because of course someone like her would. I wondered what it was like to live life without being a full-on mess, for talking to people to just be effortless, but I knew that was a pointless thing to think about because I can't change who I am and it's just depressing to wish otherwise. I was already idealizing her, I realized, and I knew that was a recipe for disaster. But I was ready to cook.

As though she could sense me watching her, she turned around and met my eyes. I waved as though I'd just got there and walked my bike across the intersection.

"Hey," I said. "I love your costume." She grinned, her perfect red lips stretching into the perfect smile.

"You too. Are you a good witch or a bad witch?"

"That depends," I said, leaning in. "Oh wait, that's a line from the movie. In that case . . . I hope you don't have any buckets of water around."

"You're safe with me," she said, lying. "At least for now."

It was like all of my nerve endings were awake and aware as she introduced me to a bunch of people whose names I immediately forgot. I was lucky to remember my own.

It felt like hours and was probably maybe fifteen minutes before the group had assembled and was ready to go. There were vampires and werewolves and Marilyn Monroe, all kinds of costumes adapted to sit atop bicycles. I got a few compliments on mine, even though it was pretty basic, and it took the edge off my nerves.

There was too much going on for Delilah and I to talk one-on-one much, but I was enjoying the people watching. She made sure to pull me into conversations with the cyclists around us as we pedaled through Indy's streets, but also gave me a little space, never letting me get lost. I couldn't help but think I could get used to this.

It was starting to get dim, being fall in Indiana and all, and everyone powered on their bike lights. I was glad I'd remembered to add new batteries to mine on the way out the door, since I hadn't actually ridden this thing in a couple years. I hoped I wouldn't get a flat tire or have anything happen that would expose my real lack of bike knowledge. I was busy enough hiding the slight burning in my thighs as we pedaled more than I'd pedaled in years.

Delilah asked me questions as we rode, simple things like what I did for fun and for a living, and then deeper things like if I was close with my family. She paid attention, like she really cared about the answers. I found out she was a VP of marketing for a global real estate firm, something I would probably have judged her for if I hadn't already been a full-on smitten kitten, because capitalism and gentrification, but then we all have to make a living. She lived in one of those expensive-looking condo buildings downtown that I always wondered how anyone could actually afford. But she was also teaching herself how to play the dulcimer, and she was really into embroidery. Maybe she could play a song for me and show me some of her artwork, she said, the next time we hung out. She was already thinking about a second date. I couldn't believe my luck.

The group stopped at a hipster dive bar and everyone headed to the patio to get a beer, leaving our bikes all leaned up against each other. She offered to get me a drink and I took her up on it, but said only if she'd let me get the next round. I didn't tell her I wasn't much of a drinker, but I figured I could just sip on it unless it was one of those high-proof IPAs that taste like rotting cloves. It was a relief when she brought me a wheat beer with a big slice of orange on the rim.

"I don't care if it's uncool these days, I love a Blue Moon-type beer," she said.

I clinked plastic cups with her and didn't say out loud that I thought she was basically the perfect woman. I took the smallest of sips and waited until she turned away in conversation to pour some of it into a planter. I was not going to screw this up by getting tipsy and saying something awkward and embarrassing.

It was full-on dark soon enough, and it felt a little Halloween-spooky as the moon glowed and shadows pooled in the corner of the bar's patio.

"What do you say we ditch this crew for a while and go have our own adventure?" She grinned at me, raising her eyebrows as though egging me on to take a dare.

"Hmm . . . what do you have in mind?" I didn't tell her that whatever it was, the answer was yes. I didn't need her to know I was just that easy.

"You'll see," she said. "Finish your beer then grab your bike and follow me." She headed toward her bike and I poured the rest of my beer into the planter before following.

We rode down a street that was mostly industrial businesses and, other than the bar, all closed for the night. No trick-or-treaters or really any other people out at all. Being alone as a woman in the dark in public can be intimidating enough, and Halloween was adding another layer of creepiness, but I tried to pretend that I was game for whatever. I wanted to ask where we were going, but I was worried that I'd sound scared and boring, so I just followed along. She cued up a Halloween playlist on the phone in her bike basket, "Monster Mash" following a song from the *Nightmare Before Christmas* soundtrack.

She stopped short next to a dark gap in the blocky, empty buildings, and looked back at me, a challenge in her grin.

"What is this?" I asked. Whatever it was, I was already not a fan, but I didn't say that. I like safety, and my body all being in one piece and not chopped up by some insane killer taking advantage of Halloween to get all slasher-y.

"Well . . ." she said. "I've always wanted to see the underground part of Pogue's Run. And I figured, since we're having so much fun together, and it's right here, and I like you . . . why not now?"

My insides didn't know what to make of that. On one hand, she liked me, oh my god. On the other, she wanted to do something that every sensible part of me warned would be a very dumb thing to do. I looked around me, but didn't see what she was talking about. We were just on an empty street with somewhat ominous trees hovering darkly behind a big, neglected parking lot.

I knew about Pogue's Run. It's a perfectly nice, respectable stream, even if there are signs all along it that warn about the potential for sewage in the water after a big rainstorm. I'd heard about the underground part, though I'd never seen it. At some point a long time ago, the brilliant city planners buried a chunk of the waterway underground so they could build all the buildings of downtown Indianapolis without all that wet stuff getting in the way. Humans are wild.

"Come on," she said, and started to walk her bike toward the trees. I hesitated, but then followed. What was I going to do, wait out there on the road by myself while my date went off and did something potentially reckless and dangerous?

When I caught up with her, Delilah was pulling her bike into the trees and leaning it against one. Just ahead there were some rickety-looking wooden steps heading down to who-knows-where.

I laughed, trying to make it seem light. "This seems like a good place to bury a body."

An expression passed over her face, something I couldn't quite understand, but which unnerved me a little. Maybe she was nervous, too. Anyone with sense should have been.

"If you don't want to have a peek, that's okay," she said. "Mind watching my bike while I do?"

Of course there was no way I could let her climb down to a dark tunnel alone. Maybe she knew that, maybe it was a bluff. Either way, I had to be game for it if I wanted to have any real chance with her. If she didn't die a horrible Halloween death, she definitely wouldn't go out with a total coward.

I leaned my bike against hers and unclipped my helmet, hanging it with its attached witch hat from the handlebars. Then I begrudgingly followed her down the stairs, wishing there was some kind of handhold, imagining falling face first down into the darkness. As we headed down I could hear a little bit of water lapping. I always find it amazing that so many waterways go right through the city and we don't see them or even think about them. There's a whole world just out of sight.

The moment I set my feet down on the ground again, I knew we shouldn't be there. I used my phone's flashlight to illuminate the concrete walls that ensconced a trickle of water, giant graffiti emblazoned across them. It felt like watching all those horror movies where you yell at the characters not to do something stupid, don't go in that room, don't split up, don't, don't, don't. I started to wonder if Delilah liking me was really worth it, if this was what it meant to date her.

"It's fine," she whispered, flashing a smile at me. "I know plenty of people who have come down here before."

"At night, and on Halloween?" I asked, trying to keep my voice from betraying that I was feeling very, very freaked out. It was weird to think that we were only a couple blocks from the bar, where people in ironic costumes were talking and laughing, and not fearing for their lives even a little. But down there it felt like a completely different reality. I couldn't wait for it to be over.

"I just want to walk in a little bit. Take a couple photos so I can show the guys we did, and then I can tease them for being too afraid to come down here on All Hallows' Eve."

I could feel my forehead wrinkle, but I knew she couldn't see me well in this light. My thoughts started whirring: Did she invite the guys from the Bike Social down here before she asked me? Was I second choice, or worse? And was I actually jealous about a bunch of dudes with questionable body odor on fixies?

If I just suck it up for a couple more minutes, I told myself, this will all be over, and we can go back to the group and finish the ride. And if she wants to go out again, maybe I can pick the activity. One that wouldn't make my blood beat so loudly in my ears.

Delilah crept toward the entrance to the tunnel, and I stuck right behind her. There wasn't a lot to see besides some graffiti and abandoned belongings. Just infrastructure trying to guide nature into a more convenient path.

We walked further in, to a point where the entrance was starting to fade from view. The water lapped around my boots, threatening to find a way in and leave me with gross, damp socks for the rest of the night. This was about it for me, I decided. I'd done my part, gone into the scary abandoned tunnel on Halloween night with a cute girl. This was enough. But then she took my hand. It was the first time we'd actually touched, and for a moment, I forgot everything around me.

Then I heard it. Some kind of a growl, though the word growl couldn't really describe the awful horribleness of that sound. It was dark and guttural, and I swear the tunnel shook a little around it.

"What . . ." was all I could get out. I turned to Delilah, gripping her fingers tightly, ready to run.

"It's okay," she whispered, holding me still.

"I don't think . . ." I started, and then she pulled her hand out of mine and knelt down, picking something up out of the darkness.

When she stood back up, there was an odd expression on her face. Before I could get any more words out she said, simply, "Sorry." Then she swung.

The chunk of concrete in her hand connected with my head with an audible thwack. I splashed down, full-body, face-first into the murky, smelly water. It spattered into my eyes and up my nose, and I tried not to inhale it. My phone and its light had fallen somewhere out of reach and I couldn't see much of anything except the stars inside my skull.

I didn't pass out. Nothing movie-like like that. I was just in a whole lot of pain. I couldn't get myself up, and even if I could have, Delilah stood there next to me, still holding her makeshift weapon. I was pretty sure she'd hit me with it again if I tried to stand up.

"Why?" was all I could get out. Delilah didn't respond. She just made a tsking sound, the kind you might use to call a cat.

The sound in the tunnel got louder, like the deep rumble was getting closer, and I definitely didn't imagine the shaking this time. Something was coming, and I was pretty sure I wasn't going to like what I saw.

I never really bought into Halloween stories of monsters and demons and angry ghosts. They always just seemed silly and fake. But as the creature came into view, I knew beyond all doubt that there was something about this day, that when they said the veil between the worlds was thinnest on Halloween night that they were absolutely right the whole time.

The tunnel was dark but somehow that didn't matter, because even from my prone position, I could see what was coming, or a little glimpse of a . . . something . . . that stretched for miles. It almost shone, but it wasn't exactly that. Maybe it was reflecting the tiny amount of light from the tunnel's edge, and from the flashlight of my rapidly drowning phone. It was like its skin, or hide, or whatever you might call the surface of this enormous creature, was covered in giant, bulbous black sequins. A disco ball demon of the deep. It was terrifying and yet I couldn't look away.

"Good evening," Delilah boomed out, her voice a little shaky. "And blessed All Hallows' Eve. You honor us with your presence."

"Ex-fucking-'scuse me?" I muttered, even though it made my wounded head ache even more.

"Hush!" Delilah ordered me. "Show some respect. You have no idea whose company you're in."

"Some asshole from Tinder in a stupid Dorothy costume and a giant sparkly worm, apparently," I retorted.

She kicked me swiftly in one side, which shot little black orbs across my vision and shut me right back up.

"My apologies, Great One," she continued. "Your sacrifice is foolish and ignorant, but will still make an appropriate gift."

Well, now I was really pissed off. It was one thing for my too-good-to-be-true Tinder date to go terribly wrong—I basically expected that. But I definitely did not expect her to offer me up to be eaten by some giant creature for . . . reasons.

"Delilah," I called, curling in on myself in case she kicked me again. "I feel like you can at least give me a little Cliff's Notes on why exactly you're feeding me to this monster."

I swear, the creature looked at me then. Its eyes were more than black. They swirled with gold and I felt like it could see inside my body and all of my thoughts at once. And maybe I imagined it but it felt like it nodded at me in a way that said yeah, she probably has a right to know. Thanks, monster who is probably about to devour me whole, I thought. You're a real one.

"Ugh, fine," Delilah said. "But I'm really busy here."

I wanted to say something sarcastic about my social calendar also being pretty darn packed, but I more wanted to know just what in the Halloween hell was happening here. Delilah cleared her throat and cracked her neck left and right.

"Here's the short version: One of the guys from my class in business school told me about this legend, one night when we all went drinking after finals. Said that's how his uncle made his millions and got his three Teslas and his chalet in Aspen, that he'd invoked an ancient underground creature that traded sacrifices for really good luck, if you went to the right spot on Halloween night."

"I didn't believe him at first, of course. It sounded like such a stupid urban legend. Since when is Indianapolis a place where magical things happen? And having to do it on Halloween just sounded like some really dumb plot. But then I lucked out and got an internship at his uncle's company. Right away, I could tell something was off. The place was basically printing money, but his uncle was a full-on idiot. Everything should have been on fire, not being *Forbes*-cover-successful. I did some deep Googling about this creature of the underground and sure enough, there are stories out there if you figure out where to look."

"Uh huh," I interrupted. "And so you were like hey, let me grab some random human and see if I can feed them to a giant disco snake and maybe then . . . profit."

"It's not like I *wanted* to sacrifice people to an otherworldly deity," she said, her tone defensive. "I'm a humanitarian. I volunteer for Big Brothers, Big Sisters! I donate blood to the Red Cross! But I can help more if I'm not broke, you know. I mean, nonprofits wouldn't survive if it wasn't for wealthy people making donations. So at the end of the day, the math works out, if you think about it."

At this point, I was over it. It was one thing if Delilah saw me on a dating app and thought eh, not for me. But it was a whole other thing for her to see me and think hey, no one is going to miss this one, let's feed her to the worm. Swipe right.

The tunnel shook as the creature moved forward, effectively ending the exposition portion of our conversation. You know in stories where people say they were frozen with fear? Yeah, I was feeling that times a thousand. My head was pounding from the whack Delilah had given it, but if this was going to be a flight or fight scenario, my pulse was prepping me to try either.

As I pulled my legs up to my belly slowly, readying my feet to launch me straight into Delilah and hopefully out of the tunnel, the beast's mouth opened, and an otherworldly, horrible roar filled the space. Its breath was acrid and smoky, like what I imagine brimfire would smell like. And then there were the teeth. They weren't just normal animal teeth, no, of course not. They were each as tall as me and sharp like needles, circling the edges of its mouth like one of those terrifying sea creatures that lives at the very, very bottom where humans should never be. I considered peeing myself.

Delilah stared, her pupils enormous. I couldn't help but smile as I realized that something was not going to plan. At least if I was going to be eaten by a giant ancient worm creature, maybe it could also inconvenience my date a little.

The bottom section of its teeth parted and a huge wooly tongue unrolled between them like a giant, wet carpet, its rounded edge landing just inches from me. I hoped it couldn't see my expression of mild disgust, because I was really hoping not to get eaten immediately.

"Delilah Ahnon!" shouted a voice that was . . . much smaller and less impressive than I would have imagined from this creature's frankly terrifying form. "Are you fucking serious?" the voice continued. It sounded like . . . a woman. A very annoyed, fairly young-ish sounding woman calling from somewhere inside.

Delilah's mouth dropped open and her eyes widened to comic book proportions. I was definitely sure now that this was not in the plan. Part of me wanted to run, and the other part wanted to pop some popcorn. But that tongue could have covered me completely without any effort at all, so biding my time seemed wise.

"Stephanie?" Delilah's voice had an edge to it. "Is that . . . you? There's no way." Scoffing, I think she was scoffing. That seemed unwise. Perhaps, I thought, she had changed course and now had a death wish.

"Oh so you do remember me," the voice continued.

I couldn't keep my mouth shut. "Sorry, but could someone fill me in on what's happening here? Or, I can excuse myself if you two would like some privacy."

The creature turned its giant head area just slightly toward me and I immediately had regrets. And then I realized: this creature was talking without using its tongue. I was no ancient creature zoologist, but that seemed weird.

"Oh, hello. I take it you're this year's sacrifice," the woman's voice called. "Welcome to the party. I was the last round. How many years has it been, now, Delilah? Three years? Four? This is not, I'm sorry to say, Delilah's first murder rodeo."

"Hold on now," Delilah protested, one hip shot out in offense. "I didn't murder anyone."

"Right," the voice continued, "you just drug us and bring us to the sewer and feed us to this gorgeously brilliant yet very complicated and also hungry creature, all so you can climb the stupid corporate ranks or whatever you do in your world of money and status and people who generally suck."

All of a sudden I'm seeing visions of that beer Delilah got me earlier, the one I barely sipped. Someone was a snake here, and it wasn't the otherworldly being taking up most of this tunnel.

"I'm Maia," I interjected, trying to project my voice into the cavern of the creature's mouth. I pushed myself up to sitting, figuring that Delilah had bigger problems now than me possibly getting away. "Nice to meet you, sort of. Or as good as it can be under the circumstances. Is there, just possibly, any chance that I am not going to be dinner tonight?"

"Sorry," the voice said. "I should introduce myself. Come a little closer to the mouth."

The laugh I let out would have been cringey if anyone I actually cared about had been around to hear it. It sounded unhinged. But then, if there was ever a time to be unhinged, this was probably right about it.

"No, I'm sorry," I retorted, continuing to inch back. "The worst Tinder date of my life is currently trying to sacrifice me to an enormous sewer critter and you're saying hey, step up to where the eating happens. This is the weirdest trap."

"What if I promise you're not going to get eaten?"

The voice seemed sincere, but my trust was, I think understandably, in short supply. "Excuse me for being skeptical here."

A sigh. Then the enormous tongue lapped forward, picking me up and somersaulting me toward its giant maw. It was spongy, hot. If I closed my eyes I could pretend I was on a spa day roller coaster. Well, if it wasn't for that smell.

A moment later I was inside the enormous mouth. It should have been pitch black in there, but small bits of light reflected off the inside of the creature's skin. I rolled off the back of the tongue and ended up face-first with the figure of a woman, maybe in her early thirties if I had to guess, half-absorbed in the lining of the creature's mouth. It reminded me of that Han Solo table in *Star Wars*, only with flesh, and she was very much awake and moving.

"Sorry for the dramatics," she said, shrugging her shoulders, "but Nessie's getting bored of all this talk and I really need to speed things along."

"Nessie?" I spluttered. "Am I inside the Loch Ness Monster right now?"

"Don't be silly," the woman said. "Nessie is much, much older and more powerful than that. That's just my nickname for her. I can't pronounce her real name with human vocal cords."

"Right." If I wasn't already dead, I was pretty sure I was going to be at any moment. And no one would ever know what happened to me. I hadn't told anyone where I was going, so afraid to jinx things. I would disappear into the belly of this thing in the Pogue's Run underground and that would be the end of my stupid, boring story. I definitely had regrets.

"Now that we're face-to-face, let me introduce myself. I'm Steph."

"Steph?" I wrinkled my forehead. "That's such a normal name for . . . all this."

"Right? Everything's so normal and uneventful, until you go on a date with Delilah Ahnon."

My jaw dropped open. "Hold on. You dated her, too? But you're also a giant worm."

"I guess she didn't love me if I was a worm," she quipped.

"What?"

"Nevermind. Anyway. We went out a couple times. Then Delilah wanted to go on a little subterranean adventure and, well . . . . Welcome to the worm party." She turned her head slightly and whispered, "I'm only kidding, Nessie."

"And now . . ." I glanced around, trying not to appear frantic and probably failing miserably. "I'm going to get digested . . . like you?"

"Well. Not necessarily." She grinned. "Not if you help me out."

"Right," I said. "What do you want me to do?"

"I want you to help me make a trade."

A rumble came from inside and I grabbed on to Steph's arms for stability as the surface below me shook like the strongest earthquake. When it stopped, I looked up into her face and she smiled. Her long, stringy blond hair framed her face. She had kind eyes and the type of strong nose I'd always admired. If she hadn't been half-submerged in the fleshy mouth wall of a worm creature, she would have been pretty cute.

"Uh," I grunted, separating myself from her, "thanks."

"So here's the deal," Steph said. "And we need to hustle because Nessie is not gonna have a lot of patience if it takes much longer than this even though *we agreed on this course of action months ago*." She shouted the last part down into the darkness of the creature's throat. I really hoped she wasn't going to make it angry.

"Right, so," she continued. "All I need you to do is make Delilah hold my hands."

I burped out a laugh. "Sorry, what? You want to hold hands with her?" This woman was bonkers. Delilah had sacrificed her and she wanted to snuggle.

"Just . . ." she rolled her eyes. "I don't have time to explain. Help me, and you can go home and pretend this was all a very weird, bad dream. Okay?"

"I . . . okay." I didn't really feel like I had much of a choice and if helping her hold hands with the worst date of my life would get me out of this mess, I figured I would do it. I couldn't afford to feel guilty, and I wasn't really sure if I would if given the chance to think about all this logically.

"Alright, Nessie," Steph called out, tapping her hands on the mouth wall behind her. "Let's go!"

The tongue slid out of the mouth again, and I could hear Delilah's yelp of surprise as it grabbed her and rolled her in to join the party.

"Hey honey," I said as she landed in a heap by my feet. "Did you miss me?"

She spluttered, furious like a cat who had just been given a bath. "This is unfair. It's breaking the terms of our deal. I brought you a sacrifice!" she screamed to the creature that surrounded us on all sides. "You are not honoring the terms and conditions of our contract!" The creature did not respond, but I did.

"Did you have it reviewed by your lawyer?" I snarked. "I wouldn't be surprised if a contract with an ancient being has a lot of caveats."

"Hi Delilah," Steph said. "It's been a long time."

Delilah looked up, horror filling her face as she took in Steph's legs and half her torso embedded in flesh. "Steph. Oh my . . . oh no. This is not at all what I thought . . ."

"You just thought I'd get eaten, the end, huh?" She laughed. "If only. But hey, it hasn't been all bad. I've made good friends with Nessie here. We've had some good conversations this past year. And she's kind of over the whole human sacrifice thing now." She petted the wall beside her and the creature shifted slightly, as though it liked being pet. Delilah's eyes widened even more.

"So then . . . if she's not going to eat one, or all of us," Delilah stammered, "can we all go?"

This time, Steph's laugh was loud and bitter. "Sweetheart. Have you seen me? Nessie's actually quite a sweetheart, and she knows a lot about magic, but even she can't reverse time. It's a little too late."

"I'm really sorry to hear that," Delilah said. "But like, you'll still let us go, right? I promise, I'm done with all this. I feel terrible."

Steph sighed loudly. "If you really felt bad, you'd do something to atone for it. Give up all the good luck and money you got by sacrificing me. Go do something that actually helps the world, like being a garbage truck driver."

"Well, I mean, I can do a lot more with what I have. I'll donate to whatever cause you want."

"Maia," Steph said. "Bring Delilah over here, please."

"No problem." I was done with Delilah's empty PR bullshit. I grabbed her around the waist and started pushing her toward Steph's outstretched hands. When she was close enough, Steph grabbed her by the wrists.

"Hi honey," she said, a smile splitting her face. "You're home."

I could feel electricity in the air as Steph held tight. Delilah started to shake. It was more than fear. Something was happening.

"Okay Nessie, I'm ready," Steph whispered. The mouth-room rumbled and Delilah let out a scream that a moment later turned into a delighted laugh. Steph's hands released and Delilah stepped back. Steph-in-the-wall pushed her hands against it, as though she was trying to wriggle out.

Meanwhile, Delilah did a little spin with a kick at the end, then looked down, admiring her ruby red sneakers. "Oh wow," she whispered, so quietly I almost missed it over the noise Steph was making. "I forgot how good it feels to move." Then she looked up, and as soon as our eyes met, I knew. Delilah wasn't Delilah anymore.

She held out her hand. "Nice to meet you again. As I said before, I'm Steph."

"You . . ." I wasn't sure what to say. I had just seen something truly magical.

"While I would prefer my own body, this one is just going to have to do. Since mine is worm food and all, and really it's only fair."

Delilah screeched from the wall, "You cannot leave me like this!"

"Don't worry," Steph retorted. "Nessie liked me, so she swallowed me as slowly as she could. I don't think you're going to have that issue."

Delilah yelled a string of profanities that was honestly impressive in its variety. Steph just smiled. She offered me her hand.

"Shall we?"

I took it, and we carefully made our way across the spongy tongue, between the parted needle teeth, and back out of the humid mouth. It snapped shut behind us with a force that made me stumble.

Steph helped me back up. She seemed nice. She turned back and hugged the giant creature as best she could. "Nessie," she said, "I think I'm going to miss you most of all."

The creature seemed to lean back, and then it slithered its sparkly disco body away back in the direction it came. We stared after it until there was no trace left.

"Well," I finally said, when I remembered how to speak. "This has been quite a night. Want to get out of here?"

Steph-in-Delilah flashed me a charming smile that was only Steph and not Delilah and we walked out of the tunnel together.

"You know," she said, as we climbed up the stairs and made our way back to our bicycles. "I think I'm going to go blond." We both grinned at that.

"Do you feel up to riding?" I asked. "I know you've had a real time."

"I cannot wait," she replied.

We got back on our bikes and started to pedal down the dimly lit street. The Bike Social group was still on the bar's patio, clustered up like they were about to head out. I couldn't have been gone all that long and yet, it had been forever.

"Hey, where have you two been?" one of the guys called, looking up and down the mess of us.

"Oh, you know," Steph called back. "Just sightseeing." She glanced over to me and bit her bottom lip in a way that made my stomach do back flips.

"Ahh . . ." He winked at her. "Gotcha. A nice night for it. Well, we're heading to the next stop in a few. You two coming with?"

"What do you think?" she asked me, and I could tell she really was leaving it up to me. It wasn't all about what she wanted, and I know that's a small thing, but also it was everything.

"I think . . ." and I smiled at her, "it's a date."

Bicycle Built for Two

Dawn Vogel

The halls of Smolton High School were abuzz with plans for the annual Halloween parade. Conceived as an alternative to potential mayhem for the town's teens, the high schoolers engaged in a friendly competition to come up with the best entry on feet, skates, skateboards, or bikes every year.

Gaby Chavez had a plan. She'd found a tandem bike while helping her grandparents clean out their garage over the summer. She'd saved up money from her part-time job to get it back in working condition, with new tires, a chain, and brake lines, all of which had seen far better days when she'd carried it out of the garage.

Now all she needed was someone to ride it with her. And there was only one person she'd considered for the job.

Regan Smith was an exchange student at Smolton for her senior year. She'd said the name of the place she was from once, on her first day, at an assembly to welcome the exchange and transfer students. Gaby couldn't recall the location (other than it sounding vaguely Scandinavian), just everything else about her. Regan was tall, with pale blond hair in a pixie cut, framing her pale face and stunning blue eyes. She was also exceptionally quiet and didn't seem to have made many friends in her first month of school, but she'd proved her intelligence in the classes Gaby had with her.

Gaby, who'd been smitten from the moment she first saw Regan, and only becoming increasingly interested as she observed more about her, had been working up the nerve to talk to Regan all month. She still wasn't sure she was ready. But she told herself it was now or never, if she wanted this tandem bike idea to work out.

She waited until the end of the day, hurrying to Regan's locker from her last period math class.

Regan wasn't there.

Gaby's heart sank. It figured she'd conquered her nerves, just for disappointment to strike. Maybe she'd have better luck tomorrow.

"Excuse me?" Regan's quiet voice grabbed Gaby's attention.

"Hi!" Gaby said, smiling broadly now that she realized she hadn't missed her chance.

"I need to get into my locker," Regan said, pointing behind Gaby.

"Right, sorry. Hey, I was actually waiting here for you."

Regan glanced up from her combination lock. "You were?"

"Yeah. Um, I'm Gaby, by the way. We have a couple of classes together."

"Yes, I've seen you in them."

Gaby thought that sounded promising—Regan had noticed her. She tried to calm her fluttering stomach before she spoke again. "So, you've heard about the big Halloween parade, right?"

Regan nodded, opening her locker and loading her books into it.

"Do you have any plans for a costume for it?"

"No, I don't. We don't really do Halloween where I'm from."

Gaby frowned. "Don't do Halloween?"

"Yeah, it's just not a big deal there."

"Oh. Well, would you be interested in being in the parade?"

Regan pulled a couple of notebooks from her locker, then looked at Gaby, biting her lip. "I don't know. It's sort of a lot, isn't it?"

"I mean, I guess. But I have an idea that needs two people to make it work."

"What's your idea?"

Gaby beamed. "I want to turn my tandem bike into a rocket ship."

"Tandem bike?"

"Yeah, it's a bike with two seats. Takes two people to pedal it. I mean, it's not, like, hard work or anything. It just doesn't work well with only one rider—" Gaby trailed off, having reached the end of her courage under Regan's continued frown.

"Okay," Regan said.

"Okay? Really?"

"Sure, a rocket ship sounds like a good costume for a tandem bike."

"Awesome! So, most people work on their costumes and stuff on the weekends. If you wanna put your number in my phone, I'll text you my address, and we can figure out a good time to meet this weekend."

Regan took Gaby's offered phone and poked at the screen, then handed it back.

Gaby tapped Regan's number and sent a text message, which was soon followed by Regan's phone buzzing. "There you go, that's me."

Regan looked at her phone and nodded. "Thank you. I'll talk to you later about our plans." Slinging her backpack over her shoulder, she made her way down the hallway, pausing just before heading outside to turn and wave at Gaby.

Gaby waved back, waiting until the door closed behind Regan to do a tiny victory dance.

Now she needed to figure out if Regan liked girls, and more specifically, her.

Gaby had peeked out the living room curtains at least a dozen times before she saw Regan approaching the house. She scrambled back into a casual posture on the couch, not wanting it to be obvious she'd been waiting and watching.

The doorbell rang, and she made herself take a deep breath, both for a momentary pause and to calm her anxiety, before opening the door.

"Hey," she said, smiling at Regan. "I'll meet you on the driveway in a minute."

Regan pointed toward the driveway. "Over there?"

"Yeah, just gonna open the garage from the inside."

"Okay."

Gaby closed the door slowly, making sure Regan was heading in the right direction, then ran through the kitchen to the door into the garage. She tapped the "open" button on the wall just beyond and was wheeling the tandem bike out toward Regan when the garage door finished its slow ascent.

Regan eyed the bike, tilting her head to one side and then the other. "That's a much longer bike than I expected."

"Yeah, the frame has to accommodate two seats." Gaby paused. "It just occurred to me to ask. You do know how to ride a bike, right?"

"Of course. Unless it's different than a standard bike."

"Not much different. Do you want to give it a try, though, before we start work on the ship? Just to get the feel for it?"

"Yes. Good idea."

Gaby went back into the garage and grabbed her bike helmet and her mom's, handing the latter to Regan. "Let me know if that one's too big, and I'll see if I can find another one."

Regan looked at the helmet, watching Gaby as she put hers on, and then followed suit. "It fits."

"Okay, but—" Gaby gestured at the chin strap, which was loose under Regan's jaw. "Let me, uh—" She approached Regan, trying not to trip over her own feet, then adjusted the strap, her fingers grazing the soft skin of Regan's neck. "There you go."

Regan touched her neck where Gaby had brushed against it, blushing as she did. "Oh. Thank you."

"You're welcome." Gaby stepped across the bike frame in front of the first seat, planting her feet on either side. "Okay, get ready like this. Then we'll both stand on the left pedal, push off from the ground with our right feet, and go."

Regan followed Gaby's instructions, and soon they were pedaling down the street. The bike wobbled a bit as they adjusted their balance, each getting accustomed to the different center of gravity when there were two riders. Then the tandem bike evened out, and they rode laps around the block, turning smoothly at the ends, and finally braking as they turned the bike back into Gaby's driveway.

"And then off in the opposite order. Right foot on the ground, then left."

"That was delightful!" Regan exclaimed, removing the helmet and handing it back to Gaby. "So now what do we do?"

"Well, my dad got me a refrigerator box to use for the body of the ship—"

"Cardboard?"

"Yeah, it's lightweight. We'll build a frame with some dowel rods."

Regan frowned. "But if we're building a spaceship, shouldn't we use metal?"

"That would be heavy, wouldn't it?"

"Aluminum wouldn't be too heavy."

"True, but unless you've got a secret pile of aluminum sheeting somewhere—" Gaby shrugged. "Anyway, it's just a costume. We're just going for the general idea."

"Ah. I see. No, I don't have any aluminum sheeting."

"So yeah, cardboard. I've got some drawings for how we can set it up. So we'll draw it, paint it, and then cut it out."

Regan nodded, though a frown still creased her brow. "And we don't need a propulsion system, because we'll pedal the bike to make it move?"

"Right, though I was thinking we could cover some paper towel rolls with aluminum foil and make some cut-outs of flames or maybe some streamers to make it look like it's flying."

"Most rockets don't—" Regan trailed off. "Ah, but I understand. It's more like a cartoon rocket than a real one."

"Yeah." Gaby grinned. "It doesn't need to look super realistic. And we'll put window holes in so we can throw candy to the kids."

"Perhaps you should show me the drawings."

"Oh, yeah. I, uh, left those in my room. Do you want to come inside with me?"

Regan looked at the tandem bike and the open garage door. "Is it okay to leave this unattended here?"

"Oh, yeah. My mom drove over to my grandma's house for a few hours, so she won't run it over or anything. My dad's watching college football, so he won't go anywhere either. And this is the suburbs. Not a lot of theft here. So yeah, it's fine."

"Okay. Let's look at the drawings."

Gaby led Regan through the house, pointing out the bathroom as they passed it, and then into her room. "Oh, sorry about the mess." She hadn't entirely thought through the plan of showing off her room. But she'd hoped it might give her a chance to gauge Regan's reaction to the pride flags and posters that hung there.

"Oh, it's very colorful," Regan said.

Gaby laughed. That was a kind way to describe the space her parents claimed 'looked like a unicorn ate too much cake and vomited everywhere.' She didn't know if Regan would understand that description. Her English was amazing, but some jokes didn't always make sense to someone who was thinking between languages.

"Um, yeah, I like a lot of colors," Gaby said, finally. "Especially rainbows."

"I also like rainbows, but we don't see them where I'm from."

"Oh, is it super cloudy when it rains? Because, you know, can't have a rainbow without rain and sun."

"Yes. That must be it."

"But no Halloween and no natural rainbows? That must suck!"

Regan bit her lip and cast her gaze down before nodding.

Gaby was sure she'd just ruined her chances by telling Regan her homeland sucked. But she picked up the drawings from her desk and sat on the end of the bed. "So, uh, here's what I've got."

Regan remained standing, as though she was waiting for Gaby to turn the paper around like a show and tell. Like she either hadn't gotten Gaby's subtle invitation to sit beside her on the bed, or she wasn't interested in doing so.

Gaby tried not to let the disappointment show on her face as she turned the drawing toward Regan. "So yeah, it's sort of like an old space shuttle design, but a little more streamlined like a bullet train."

"Very aerodynamic. I think that will work well for the bike."

"Great, then I guess we should get started back out in the garage."

Regan looked at the pride paraphernalia on Gaby's walls, then back at Gaby. "What if we had the, uh, tailpipes with rainbow streamers instead of fire?"

"Oh, that's perfect!" Gaby grinned and scribbled a note on her design.

With the cardboard portion of the ship done, the following weekend was slated to build the dowel-rod structure to keep the cardboard in place and far enough to either side of the tandem bike so they could pedal and steer it. Gaby had drawn it up and run it past her dad, who had given her a few tips on minimizing the number of dowel rods and the best ways to keep them in place.

Gaby was outside, putting the first dowel rods into place, when Regan arrived, right on schedule, pulling a rolling suitcase behind her.

"Coming over to spend the night?" Gaby joked.

Regan's eyes widened as she looked down at the suitcase. "Oh, no. I just needed to carry some additions I thought of. Unless I was supposed to spend the night?"

"No, I was just joking, because it's a suitcase. What kind of additions?"

"Well, we made the sides and front of the ship, but nothing to go over our heads or on the back. So I found a silver crushed taffeta tablecloth we can drape across the top, and it's long enough to cover part of the back as well, without being so long it would get tangled in the rear wheel."

"Nice!"

"I got my own helmet, too, but you might have to help me with the straps again." Regan blushed as she had when Gaby had helped her with the helmet previously, but pulled her helmet from the suitcase, showing off a rainbow sticker running down the center from the front to back.

"Oh, I love the sticker!" Gaby exclaimed. "Where'd you find that?"

"One of the younger daughters of my host family gave it to me from her collection."

"Very cool."

"I also found rainbow streamers." Regan held those up and smiled. "For the tailpipes."

"You've thought of everything. I'm so glad I asked you to ride in the parade with me."

"So am I. I enjoy riding a bicycle here. The wind on my face is—" She trailed off, as if at a loss for words, but she placed her hand on her cheek and beamed. "Oh, but we won't feel the wind on our faces when we have the ship costume over the bike, will we?"

"Only a little bit, because we have to keep the front open so we can see. But we'll have to ride slowly for the parade." Gaby hesitated. "If you'd like, we could go for a longer ride another time, without the costume."

Regan smiled broadly, flashing stunning white teeth between her lips, though Gaby was focused more on the latter. "Yes, I'd love that!"

"Cool, it's a date," Gaby said, hazarding a wink at Regan.

Regan looked confused for only a moment before emulating Gaby's wink.

Gaby and Regan sat within the confines of the spaceship costume amongst the crowd of teens on bikes, skateboards, and skates. Someone ahead of them was even on stilts, though Gaby couldn't tell who it was under the cartoonish papier-mâché skeleton costume. The air buzzed with excitement as the assembled students waited for the announcement to begin the parade.

Gaby looked back at Regan. "Ready for this?"

"Yes. When do we start?"

"Please give a warm welcome to the students of Smolton High School!" blared a voice over the PA system.

"Sounds like now!"

The two girls pedaled forward, keeping their speed slow as everyone got moving. Within a couple of minutes, they saw the first of the costumed kids lining Main Street, plastic jack-o'-lanterns and pillowcases ready to fill with candy. Gaby and Regan had strapped bags filled with candy to both sets of handlebars on the tandem bike, ready to toss out the small windows of the spaceship.

One little boy, dressed as an astronaut, cheered loudly when he saw their costume. "Spaceship!" He pointed at them as he tugged on his mom's jacket sleeve. "They made a spaceship, Mom!"

Regan laughed. "Wow, they really like this parade!"

Gaby laughed too. "Yep, it's pretty fun for everyone."

The parade continued at a snail's pace. It wasn't uncommon for things to stop entirely, so Gaby kept a close eye on the high schoolers ahead of them for any sign they might need to slow even more or stop the tandem bike.

She frowned, though, when she spotted the parade turning onto Jackson Street. "Did you hear anything about the parade route?" she asked Regan.

"I didn't pay much attention. I don't know my way around town very well."

"I didn't either, because it's always been the same route—down Main Street to Smolton Park. But we're turning left up ahead."

"There are some flashing lights ahead. Are they emergency lights?"

Gaby blinked at the blue and red lighting up the block ahead, then nodded. "Yeah, I think so. That must be what's going on."

The person on the stilts, though, didn't seem to have noticed the change in route. They teetered dangerously as one of their stilts ran into one of the parked police cars barricading the far side of the intersection, and their arms pinwheeled as they started falling backward, toward the parade entries behind them.

Toward Gaby and Regan.

"Oh, crap," Gaby said, jerking the handlebars to the right in an attempt to get out from under the falling stilt walker.

The bike wobbled, tilting too far to the right . . .

And Gaby's view changed.

Instead of the falling papier-mâché skeleton and the police lights, the sky was deep indigo above a rust-colored landscape of sand dunes and mountains. No breeze and no smells reached her, almost as though she'd ridden into a painting.

"What?" Gaby gasped.

The bike was still moving forward, even though Gaby had stopped pedaling. It wobbled again, and Regan cried out, "Gaby!"

But Gaby couldn't respond. Her breath caught in her chest, her pulse raced, and cold sweat sprang up across her body. She slumped along with the bike as it fell to the side, stirring up a dusty cloud.

The cardboard spaceship shifted as it collided with the ground. Gaby's hands clenched into fists, and she dug her fingernails into her palm, as her jaw worked up and down with no sound coming out.

"Gaby?" Regan appeared in Gaby's narrowed field of vision. "Gaby, what's wrong?"

Gaby just gaped at the sky, the sandy dirt, and now at Regan.

Regan helped Gaby to her feet, then stood with her hands on Gaby's shoulders, looking into her eyes. "Gaby?"

Gaby blinked, the gentle pressure of Regan's touch pulling her back to herself. "Where are we?"

"I'm sorry, I panicked," Regan said. "I didn't want the person on the stilts to fall on us and crush us, so I . . . I moved us out of the way."

"But to where?" Gaby asked, her voice taking on the edge of a panicked whine.

Regan said a word so far from Gaby's comprehension that she wasn't even able to parse it.

"I don't . . . where is that?"

"It's where I'm from." Regan bit her lip and looked away from Gaby. "I'm sorry. I lied." She let go of Gaby's shoulders and took a step backward. "I understand if you're upset."

Gaby reached out for Regan's hand. "Wait, don't go. I'm having a panic attack. It happens sometimes. Can you . . . will you hold my hand for a minute?"

Regan nodded and stepped closer, taking Gaby's hands between both of hers.

Back in contact with Regan, Gaby took a deep breath and blew it out slowly. After a few rounds of that, she made eye contact with Regan again. "Okay, tell me again where we are?"

Regan said the same word again. "It's my home planet. I'm not from wherever Scandahoovia is. I just let people believe that because I didn't think they'd let me go to your school if I said I was an alien."

"Alien. You're an alien." Gaby grinned. "No way!"

"You're not upset?"

"Upset? No. A little confused still, sure. But also, holy crap! I'm on another planet!"

"Yes. That's not bad?"

"No," Gaby said immediately. "Well, maybe. I mean . . . I really don't know."

"Oh." Regan's gaze slid away from Gaby's face and to the sandy terrain beneath their feet.

"No, it's okay. I just don't know how to get back to Smolton. But I guess if you could get us here, you can get us back, too, right?"

"Yes, but I probably shouldn't go back now."

"Why not?"

"Because if everyone finds out I'm an alien, they'll probably kick me out of school, out of my host family's house, everything."

Gaby pursed her lips. "So what if we don't tell anyone?"

"Why wouldn't you tell everyone?"

"Because . . ." Gaby paused. "Because I want you to be able to come back to Smolton."

"But why?"

"Because I like you, Regan. I mean, I like you, like you."

Regan's eyes widened. "You do?"

"Yeah. I guess you might not have noticed, since you're not from Earth. But that's okay. I still like you."

"I thought you were upset because I dragged you halfway across the galaxy, and you didn't want to be here with me. Because you said where I came from must suck, with no Halloween or natural rainbows."

Gaby shook her head, squeezing Regan's hands in hers. "No, I didn't mean it like that. I just really like Halloween and rainbows. I don't think I'd want to live here, but I wouldn't want to visit halfway across the galaxy with anyone else."

"Oh, I understand. And I do like being on Earth. Especially because that's where you live." Regan blushed, though she didn't look away from Gaby.

Gaby bit her lip. "Is it okay if I kiss you?"

Regan's eyes grew wide again, but she nodded. "Yes."

Gaby leaned in and kissed Regan gently. A spark zapped both of them, and they pulled away from each other, fingers flying to their respective lips.

"Try it again," Regan whispered around her fingers.

Gaby did, this time without the electrical jolt. Or, at least without the painful shock. This time, their lips met, soft and inviting, and they both leaned into the kiss.

"High electricity content here, on account of the sand," Regan said, blushing as she pulled away from Gaby's second kiss.

"That's okay." Gaby twined her fingers with Regan's. "But the second one was better."

"Yes, I think so, too. But I suppose we should focus on getting back to Smolton. And then we can continue trying to kiss even better."

"I like the sound of that. So what's next?"

Regan looked at the bike, and Gaby followed her gaze. Both tires were flat, and the chain had slipped off the gear's teeth on one side.

"Oh, no," Gaby said. "Let me guess, we need that to get home?"

"We do. But . . ." Regan gestured to one of the nearest dunes. "My parents live in a town that way. They'll have tools we can use to repair the bike. And then, we can ride from there back to Smolton. In a blink, I mean. Not the whole distance."

Gaby grinned. "And no one in Smolton will probably notice we vanished, with all of the chaos of the parade. If anyone asks, we can tell them we took an alternate route so we could have some privacy."

"Do you think that will be believable?" Regan asked.

"Yeah, I think so. Your parents won't mind that you brought someone from Earth home with you?"

"On the contrary. They're going to be so excited to meet someone from Earth. Especially if she's my girlfriend."

Gaby forced herself not to shout with joy at Regan's suggestion. Instead, she grinned from ear to ear and squeaked out an "Awesome" as they picked up the tandem bike and cardboard spaceship costume together and started for Regan's parents' house.

About the Authors

N. Anaar is a professional hacker and tinkerer. In her free time, she enjoys the outdoors, cozy books, and the creation and consumption of food. "Clocks" is her first published work.

Elly Bangs is the author of the apocalyptic cyberpunk collective-consciousness novel *UNITY*, as well as numerous short stories appearing in *Lightspeed Magazine*, *Clarkesworld Magazine*, *Beneath Ceaseless Skies*, and elsewhere. She lives in Seattle, where she fixes machines and rides a bicycle a long long way. Find more of her work at elbangs.com.

Siri Caldwell writes contemporary and paranormal lesbian romance and is a Lambda Literary Award finalist. Whether they're ghosts, mermaids, or plain old humans, her characters lead lives where, despite marginalization and alienation, love and a sense of belonging are possible.

Erin Cullen is a writer and neuroscience researcher living in New York City. She thanks the organizers of the Burlington VT Queen City boombox glitter rides for inspiring this story.

Grace Desmarais is a cartoonist and illustrator based in Brooklyn, New York. She draws fantasy-romance comics with a hint of spice. When she's not making comics, Grace is busy re-playing Dragon Age and reading romance novels. Find more of her work on Instagram: @gracedesmarais.

Kay Hanifen was born on a Friday the 13th and once lived for three months in a haunted castle. So, obviously, she had to become a horror writer. Her work has appeared in over one hundred anthologies and magazines. Her first anthology as an editor, *Till the Yule Log Burns Out*, was published in 2024. When she's not consuming pop culture with the voraciousness of a vampire at a 24-hour blood bank, you can usually find her with her black cats or at kayhanifenauthor.wordpress.com, Twitter: @TheUnicornComi1, and Instagram: @katharinehanifen.

Nell Hanson is a fiction writer specializing in horror and speculative fiction. They graduated in 2018 from the University of North Carolina at Wilmington with a Bachelor of Arts in creative writing. They are deeply interested in the stranger aspects of life as well as the unknown aspects of death, which is reflected in their work.

Valerie Hunter teaches high school English and has an MFA in writing for children and young adults from Vermont College of Fine Arts. Her stories have appeared in publications including *Beneath Ceaseless Skies*, *Capsule Stories*, *OFIC*, and *Sonder*, as well as multiple anthologies.

Summer Jewel Keown is a Midwestern fiction writer, with stories in previous *Bikes in Space* installments, including *CATS: Cycling Across Time & Space* and *Bikes Not Rockets*. She has two sapphic romance novels published under the name Sofi Keren. Chat her up on Bluesky: @janeire.bsky.social or at medusafish.com.

Jessie Kwak is an author and business book ghostwriter living in Portland, Oregon. She is the author of thrillers and space scoundrel sci-fi crime novels, along with a handful of productivity books including *From Chaos to Creativity* and *From Big Idea to Book*. You can find more at jessiekwak.com.

Mildred Locke is a Sheffield-based bike media journalist, fiction writer, and webcomic creator. In addition to sci-fi and horror short stories, she writes historical fiction and is currently working on her first novel. You can find her personal essays at mildredwrites.substack.com, and her queer webcomic, "Limelight," at tapas.io/series/LimelightStory/info.

Kortney Nash is a writer and editor based in New Jersey. She has a short story featured in the horror anthology *The Black Girl Survives in this One*, and a picture book titled *Tell Me About Juneteenth* illustrated by DeAndra Hodge. When not writing, she can be found cross stitching or watching cartoons. Connect with her on Twitter: @quarrtknee.

Dawn Vogel has loved Halloween for as long as she can remember, and she especially loves reading and writing about the spooky season. She lives in Seattle with her husband, author Jeremy Zimmerman, and their herd of cats. Visit her at http://historythatneverwas.com.